HELLF ＿

Hellfire's outlaw gang raided a train bound for Calamity and carrying fifty thousand dollars. But Marshal Lincoln Hawk thwarted their plans and, in the chaos, eighteen innocent townsfolk were killed and the money went missing.

Sixteen years later, a vengeful Hellfire escapes from prison and goes in search of the missing money. But in the now abandoned Calamity, Marshal Hawk has appointed himself as Hellfire's judge, jury and executioner and is waiting for him.

Can either of them discover what happened to the money? And who is the ghostly figure haunting the station? Only one thing is certain – when the gunsmoke clears just one man will be left standing.

By the same author

Lincoln Hawk
Ambush in Dust
    Creek
Golden Sundown
The Man They
    Couldn't Hang
Hellfire
Raiders of the
    Mission San Juan
The Butcher of
    Hooper's Creek
Siege at Hope Wells
Ride the Savage
    River
The Red Plains
    Avenger
The Honor of the
    Badge
Reckoning at El
    Dorado

Palmer & Morgan
Escape from Fort
    Benton
To The Death
Stand-off at Copper
    Town

The Redemption Trail
Dead Men Walking
Straight to Hell
The Land of Lost
    Dreams

Standalone
Silver Gulch Feud
Showdown in Dead
    Man's Canyon
Clearwater Justice
Quick on the Draw
Return to Black Rock
A Man Rode into
    Town
Last Stage to
    Lonesome
Coltaine's Revenge
Kendrick's Word
Blood Gold
The Man in Black
The Sons of Casey
    O'Donnell
High Noon in Snake
    Ridge
The Hangrope Posse
Shot to Hell

HELLFIRE

SCOTT CONNOR

CULBIN PRESS

First published in 2006 by Robert Hale Limited
Copyright © 2004, 2016, 2018 by Scott Connor
ISBN: 9798595740159

Published by Culbin Press.

ONE

The fire was already raging out of control. Only minutes after Sheriff McCarthy had heard the prisoners' first cries of alarm the flames had become an inferno and converted the small jailhouse into a hellish place of death.

Earlier that day he had received a consignment of prisoners, all of them lifers, who were being transferred to a new prison. No matter how worthless these men were, the lawman reckoned that their panicked cries would fuel his nightmares for years.

Deputy Lynch joined him, still shrugging into his clothes, and the two lawmen faced the building. As the flames erupted before them, ensuring that neither man could get within twenty feet of the jailhouse, the sheriff pulled his deputy back.

"It's hopeless," he said.

"It is, but we have to do something," Lynch said.

"There's nothing we can do but pray for their souls and make sure the fire doesn't spread beyond the compound."

In that they were lucky, the jailhouse was on the edge of Lester Forks and at least fifty yards beyond the nearest building.

"Have you got any idea how it started?" Lynch asked.

With an arm up to shield his face from the heat, McCarthy shrugged.

"No, but perhaps one of the prisoners tried a wild scheme to escape and it went wrong."

"Or it didn't and this is to cover up his escape."

McCarthy nodded, already dreading the search through the wreckage for bodies when the fire died down.

"I reckon we should. . . ."

McCarthy flinched as the jailhouse door rattled and then flew open. A prisoner hurtled through. His clothes were ablaze and flames trailed behind him. With frantic gestures, he tugged at his jacket and threw it to the ground, but smoke still plumed from his shirt and he dropped and then rolled in the dirt.

The two lawmen broke into a run and joined him. McCarthy grabbed his shoulders while Lynch kicked dirt over him.

"I'm obliged," the prisoner said, still squirming within his smoldering clothing.

"Are any more in there alive?" McCarthy asked, while Lynch stamped on the man's discarded jacket.

"There is," a voice intoned from behind him.

McCarthy started to turn, but at that moment the man on the ground took advantage of the distraction to leap up. His hand closed on McCarthy's holster and tore out his gun. Within a moment McCarthy found that the man had his own gun on him.

He raised his hands, but that didn't concern him as much as the steady footfalls from behind. He turned. Silhouetted against the burning jailhouse stood a man, his legs astride and smoke rising from his clothes.

Behind him, two other prisoners scampered out. One man smacked his jacket against the ground to extinguish the burning cloth while the other man slapped his arms and legs as if he were engaging in a wild dance. The central man appeared oblivious to the smoke rising from his hat and clothes as he faced McCarthy, his eyes twinkling.

"You set the jailhouse alight, didn't you?" McCarthy said.

"I sure did," the man said, his voice light and unconcerned by the screaming still ripping out from the building behind him.

"Who are you?"

The man strode toward McCarthy, as stray tendrils of smoke spiraled away in his wake. He had a wide mark on his cheek, perhaps a birthmark, and eyes that burned with savage malevolence. He stomped to a halt and, with a casual gesture, flipped his smoldering hat to the ground.

"They call me Hellfire," he said. "You're about to find out why."

*   *   *

"What do you want?" Harvey Baez asked.

Before him, the three men stood before the trading post door, the early-evening breeze rippling their long coats. With slow, deliberate paces, they strode to the counter and lined up.

"Shelton Baez," the lead man said through gritted teeth.

"Who wants. . . ?" Harvey gulped to loosen his tight throat as a cold fire flared the man's eyes. "I'll go fetch him."

He edged back a pace and then hurried into the storeroom while demanding that his uncle come quickly.

"Sort this out yourself," Shelton said and waved in a dismissive manner at him while continuing to count his stock.

"I haven't seen these customers before." Harvey pointed back into the main room. "They don't look like they want to buy anything, if you know what I mean."

Shelton snapped up to stand straight and closed his eyes for a moment.

"What do they look like?"

"Three men, surly, long coats."

"Any of them got a mark on his face?"

"Nope."

Shelton sighed and placed a hand to his chest. "Then go outside."

"And do what?"

"Just go!" Shelton grunted. He brushed past Harvey and into the store, his back straight and his eyes blank.

Harvey edged away, but then wavered and then shuffled back across the storeroom to stand in the doorway.

"You came quickly," Shelton said.

"We don't waste time," one of the new-comers replied. "Who have you got?"

"His given name is Jeremiah Court, but he goes by the name of. . . ." Shelton turned toward the door, but Harvey had anticipated his move and stepped back. "They call him Hellfire."

Giddiness reeled Harvey back against the wall. His guts rumbled and he had to gulp to fight down the bile that burned his throat.

"I've never heard of him," the man said.

"He's spent the last sixteen years in prison, but three weeks ago they tried to transport him to a new prison. He escaped."

The first twinge of a potential headache throbbed as Harvey shuffled back into the doorway.

"We charge five hundred dollars." The man leaned on the counter and raised his eyebrows. "Can you afford that?"

"Keep Hellfire away from me, permanently, and I'll pay you one thousand."

When the man received nods from his colleagues, he smiled.

"Then you just hired us. When are you expecting this Hellfire?"

Shelton shivered. "It could be any day, perhaps even tonight."

Harvey wanted to hear more, but two of the men wandered around the post. He darted back from the doorway and left the storeroom through the back exit. Outside, he sat on the old dug-out and faced west toward the railroad and the town of Stark Pass, the trading post's nearest settlement now that Calamity had been abandoned. The dying sun was dipping below the far mountains, bleeding deep red rays across the land and stretching long shadows away from every boulder.

"One thousand dollars," he said to himself. "One zero zero zero. There can't be that much money in the whole world."

As the last sliver of sun faded away, he tried to keep his mind from dwelling on the fear that these men's arrival and Shelton's mention of Hellfire had instilled in him. Then Shelton shouted some orders at him from inside, so he stood up and walked around to the front of the post to care for the men's horses.

To his side, something moved. Harvey

flinched, but when he turned, all was still. He squinted as he faced the ridge that loomed over the trading post, but nobody was visible. Then the movement came again and Harvey jerked his head around to confront it.

A half-mile down the ridge, on the edge of a rocky outcrop, a solitary figure stood, the form standing out in sharp relief against the red sky. With his eyes narrowed to slits, Harvey reckoned it was a slight person, perhaps a woman, a cape wrapped around her, the trailing ends fluttering behind her in the breeze.

He blinked hard to ensure the figure wasn't just a burst of sun-blindness, and when he re-opened his eyes the figure had gone. Harvey bit back his flash of disappointment and smiled.

"You're back," he said to himself.

TWO

U.S. Marshal Lincoln Hawk drew his horse to a halt. Hunched forward in the saddle, he faced what was left of the town. The moment he had heard that Hellfire had escaped he knew that he had to be the one who tracked him down, but with Hellfire covering his tracks, nobody had gotten a lead on him.

Lincoln reckoned he knew where Hellfire would go, so he'd gone directly to Calamity, but his destination was as unrewarding as he'd feared. The last decade hadn't been kind to the town.

The moldering remnants of what could have been a fine town were now a festering sore beside the railroad. The buildings that still stood were shells, hinting only at their former glory.

The boardwalks had rotted. The standing structures teetered. The signs that once proudly advertised the stores and saloons had faded and dangled from rusting nails. None of the buildings' wood had been salvaged to build elsewhere, but then again, after what had happened here, Lincoln wasn't surprised.

Ahead of his deputies, Alvin Buckfast and Daniel Samuels, Lincoln rode through the dusty ghost town and stopped in front of the burned-out remnants of the train station, the original heart of the town, and then its death.

Here Lincoln dismounted and walked to the edge of the platform. He bowed his head as he strode over the rotting wood to stand beside the railroad. With his legs planted wide apart, he faced down the tracks, as if awaiting a train – just as he'd done sixteen years ago.

Alvin and Daniel lingered behind him. Then they nudged each other and Alvin shuffled across the platform to join him.

"What happened here?" he asked.

Lincoln faced the wrecked station and a main drag that should be bustling and prosperous, searching for the memories that rarely came these days while fighting back the memories that would never leave him.

"Hellfire happened," he said.

Then he walked over the tracks to stand on the very same spot on which he and Marshal Billy Epstein had stood that day.

* * *

"You're not doing that, Lincoln," Billy had said to him, his sneering expression and steadfast refusal to listen to advice as fresh today in Lincoln's memory as it had been on that fine summer evening.

"We've got no choice," Lincoln said.

He had worked for the railroad back then and had no right to order a town marshal around. As that lawman was acting like an idiot, he thought it was time for someone with sense to take control.

Earlier that day an outlaw gang led by Jeremiah Court, also known as Hellfire, had ridden into town and raided the train when it'd pulled up at the station. Hellfire reckoned $50,000 was being transported on it.

When he didn't find the money he had held everyone who had been awaiting the train hostage and given the railroad twelve hours to come up with the money. Twelve hours passed after that ultimatum and although the money was piled in a cage behind the train Marshal Epstein had taken it upon himself to call Hellfire's bluff.

"We've got every choice," Billy said. "We've got him trapped in there and we can wait him out."

"We can't. Give him the money, or give him a way out, but don't sit him out or innocent people are going to die."

As the marshal shook his head, the acrid taint of burning assailed Lincoln's nostrils. Lincoln edged out from behind the train and then winced. Tendrils of smoke were spiraling up from the station roof and a flame flickered at one of the windows.

"Hellfire's torched the station," Billy said. "Why would he do that?"

"Because the twelve hours are up, as I've been telling you, and because burning the station down is precisely what he'd do."

Billy sneered. "How would you know that?"

"They call him Hellfire. There has to be a reason."

Billy rubbed his chin as he rocked from foot to foot. In that moment Lincoln decided that if all lawmen were as ineffectual as this one, he'd consider becoming one himself. That was for another day, and now the station roof was alight and the shooting was starting.

While the marshal ordered his deputies to stay back and see what Hellfire did next, Lincoln hurried away from the train. Billy called him back, but he ignored him and continued running.

He aimed to get square on to the station and run in from the side where there were no windows. Then he could try to get into the building and get the hostages out; but as he closed on the station three men burst out from the back of the building.

Two gawping members of the townsfolk were loitering on Calamity's main drag and the outlaws cut them down. Then they ran for their horses. To Lincoln's left, Hellfire's men were trying to escape and to his right, the station was ablaze.

Despite the draw of getting into the station, he ran toward the men. On the run, he tore an arc of gunfire into them, cutting one man off with a shot to the side, and then slicing through the next two.

These men stumbled on for a few paces and then flopped to the ground to lie face down. Lincoln ran on, reloading as the other outlaws ventured out on to the platform. One outlaw turned to Lincoln and fired wildly.

Then he hunkered down to take more careful aim, so Lincoln threw himself to the ground to lie on his belly. With his gun thrust out, he slammed the man to the ground with a high shot to the neck.

He rolled again, coming to his feet, and set off. When he was just twenty feet from the station, two outlaws gained their horses, but then at last the marshal acted. With his deputies around him, he surged around the other side of the station and lay down a burst of gunfire that spooked the horses and kept the outlaws from making a run for it.

Then Hellfire appeared. He was scooting along the side of the station, keeping under the eaves, the flames shooting out from the windows and door around him, but a burst of gunfire from one of the marshal's deputies forced him to retreat.

Lincoln side-stepped behind the side of the station and waited, the heat from the fire inside already permeating the wall and warming his back. Long seconds passed, every heartbeat only helping to erode Lincoln's belief that waiting was the right thing to do, but Lincoln got his reward when Hellfire hurried out on his side of the station and he had his back to him.

"Reach," Lincoln ordered, stepping out behind Hellfire

Hellfire turned at the hip, his gun arcing around to aim at Lincoln, so Lincoln blasted a single shot, snatching the gun from his hand. Then he advanced on him, but Hellfire sneered, his hands half-raised.

"Go on," he said without a trace of fear in his eyes. "Shoot."

"I'm not doing that," Lincoln said. "I reckon the rest of your men will fight until nobody comes out of there alive, but one word from you and they'll give up."

Hellfire licked his lips. "And the deal if I help you?"

"I'm not a lawman. I can't offer no deal, but I reckon it'll sound better for you if you give yourself up."

Hellfire shrugged. "No deal."

Lincoln winced. Then, as he saw nothing in Hellfire's eyes to suggest he'd ever cooperate, he dragged him away from the burning station to get him into the custody of the marshal's deputies.

As he edged back across the platform the shooting continued in sporadic bursts from the other side of the station. Even some distance from the fighting Lincoln could see that Marshal Epstein had placed his men in all the wrong places.

They weren't giving Hellfire's men any problems, but the fire was. It had now taken hold of most of the station and if Lincoln and the ineffectual lawman didn't end this siege quickly, a lot of people were about to die.

Lincoln gained a tighter grip of Hellfire's shoulders and sped his journey across the platform, but when he reached the train none of the deputies were there. So he searched for a place to secure Hellfire while he rejoined the fighting.

Then he came across something that rocked him back on his heels – the cage and the $50,000 was no longer there. Lincoln assumed that one of the deputies had found a safer place for the money, so he found a rope and secured Hellfire.

Then he hurried over to join the marshal, now turning his thoughts to how they could end this ambush with the hostages coming out alive, but he was already too late. Neither did anyone find the missing money. . . .

* * *

In the present, Lincoln shook himself, freeing his thoughts from those events and turned to Alvin.

"I caught Hellfire, but his gang escaped. By then, the station was ablaze and we couldn't get in. They'd tied everyone up and eighteen people burned to death. It took some months, but we tracked down every last one of his gang. Hellfire never got the justice he deserved."

Alvin winced. "Why?"

"He claimed the fire broke out when his woman, Adele, accidentally knocked over an oil-lamp." Lincoln paced over the tracks and back on to the platform. "The only hostage to survive was Shelton Baez, and he didn't see how the fire started."

Lincoln continued walking across the platform. When he reached the edge he moved on for another ten steps. He turned, measuring the distance to the station. This was where he'd held Hellfire at gunpoint, but he'd let him live to get real justice.

Although that failure to receive justice was the one last spur he'd needed to become a lawman, he had never forgotten Hellfire. Lincoln turned, dismissing that day from his mind, and headed to his horse, his deputies trailing behind him.

"Afterward they didn't rebuild the station?" Alvin said.

"Nobody had the guts to carry on after that big a tragedy. The station moved down the track and Stark Pass grew up, leaving Calamity to die."

Alvin nodded, but behind them, Daniel screeched a warning. He drew his gun and turned at the hip to aim his gun at the station. Alvin and Lincoln both drew their guns and dashed back to join him. The three men stood in a defensive circle, their guns aimed around the deserted ghost town.

"What did you see?" Alvin asked from the corner of his mouth.

Daniel faced the ruined station and narrowed his eyes.

"Somebody's moving around in there."

Lincoln turned. The only movement in the wrecked skeleton of the building came from a trapped rag flicking in the wind.

"Nobody's lived in Calamity for years."

"Except for ghosts," Alvin said. He smirked and put on a false, high voice. "Maybe one of them might come out of the station and—"

Daniel shivered. "Don't mock me. When that much death happens, the ghosts never leave."

"Spare me your spooky tales," Lincoln snapped and swung his gun back into his holster. "I don't believe in that nonsense. I worry more about the living ghosts."

THREE

The man appeared to have blood splattered over his face, but Marshal Cooper noted that the bartender was trying not to stare.

"Whiskey," the man said.

The bartender swung a whiskey bottle on to the counter and sloshed a full glass, again taking the opportunity to appraise the man. From his position at the end of the bar Cooper decided that the blood wasn't fresh.

It was a blemish, perhaps an old burn, which covered most of his right cheek and spread out beneath the eye. Then that eye twitched and the bartender lowered his head.

"See anything interesting?" The man ripped back his hat and thrust his face to the side, his cheek held high. "Want to stare some more at my mark?"

"I'm sorry," the bartender said. "Have the first drink on me."

The man snorted and hurled a handful of coins on to the bar.

"I'm not looking for your pity." He turned and leaned back against the bar, facing the saloon door.

Outside, at least a dozen men were lined up at the hitching rail. Most stayed mounted, leaving three men to clump on to the boardwalk and file in through the batwings. With a swaggering gait, they headed to the bar. Cooper swirled his whiskey as the men stomped to a halt.

"Whiskeys for you three," the bartender said, beaming. "If you like what you drink, maybe you'll enjoy a longer stay."

The man with the blemish snorted and swung around.

"Quit the talk. I want Shelton Baez."

"Shelton Baez," the bartender intoned, scratching his forehead.

Cooper downed his whiskey and walked down the bar. He sized up the newcomers, and he didn't like what he saw.

"We've never heard of him," Cooper said.

The man gulped his whiskey and swirled the dregs.

"He worked with another good-for-nothing runt, Lincoln Hawk, at the railroad office in Calamity."

"There hasn't been anything like that in Calamity since . . ." Cooper rubbed his chin as he considered. ". . . fifteen years ago. Railroad office is here now, so you might try—"

"I'm not interested in asking them. I *am* asking you."

"Nope. I still don't know him."

A snarl from the blemished man encouraged the other men to stand around Cooper. They raised their heels so that they could tower over him. One man brushed imaginary dust from Cooper's shoulders, and the man who was out of Cooper's eye-line snorted a laugh at nothing in particular.

Cooper just folded his arms and kept his stance casual, but from his table in the corner Brock Crowthers was heading to the bar, leaving his drinking partner to scrape back his chair and watch him with interest.

"You're looking for Shelton Baez, you say?" Brock said, swinging to a halt. He gave a gap-toothed smile.

"Yeah."

Brock tapped his white-bristled chin, his brow furrowed with mock effort.

"The name sounds mighty familiar," he mused. Brock licked his lips, and then nodded at the whiskey bottle on the bar and grinned hopefully. "But I can't remember much when I'm right thirsty."

The man reached down the bar to finger the whiskey bottle and then scraped it along the bar to just out of Brock's reach.

"Tell me where he is and you get the rest of the bottle."

"Make it a full bottle and it's a deal." Brock shrugged. "It's a mighty long story."

"You got yourself a deal."

"Brock," Cooper urged, but Brock's whoop of delight drowned him out.

"Who wants him?" Brock said, grinning.

The man licked his lips. When he spoke he uttered his single word with an exaggerated movement of the mouth.

"Hellfire."

Cooper threw his hand to his holster, but the man who was standing behind him grabbed his arm and yanked it halfway up his back. In a skipped heartbeat Brock paled, but even as his mouth was falling open, the blemished man, Hellfire, lunged.

He grabbed Brock's collar and dragged him up close. Then he cocked his head to the side, displaying his blemish.

"I was just dragging out a yarn to get me a drink," Brock babbled. His scrawny neck bulged as he gave a pronounced gulp. "I don't know nothing about no—"

"You were, were you?" Hellfire drew his gun and thrust the barrel under Brock's chin.

"There's no need for threats," Cooper said.

"If Brock says he doesn't know where this Shelton is, he doesn't."

With a mocking shake of the head, Hellfire admonished Cooper and then turned to Brock.

"I haven't got time for you to tell me no long story." Hellfire thrust the barrel deep into Brock's flesh, forcing him up on to tip-toes. "So tell me where I can find Shelton."

"Like you said, he worked for the railroad, but that was years ago," Brock said. He flashed a desperate grin. "Then he moved on. The last I heard he was running this trading post."

"Where?"

"I don't know."

"Wrong answer." Hellfire squeezed the trigger, blasting Brock's head up and away from him, his bloodied body dead before it hit the floor.

Cooper struggled, but the man holding him wrapped his arm around his neck so tightly it closed his windpipe. As he fought for breath, the bartender ran for the door.

One of Hellfire's men ripped a bullet into his hip, which knocked him sideways for a pace.

Then he followed through with a second slug to the head that made the bartender stumble and crash through the window. Before the shards of glass had clattered to the ground outside, Brock's drinking partner jumped to his feet.

He hurled his hand to his gun, but as he dragged it from its holster Hellfire thundered a low slug into his chest which made him stagger back against the wall. The man righted himself. With grim determination he returned a shot that whistled by Hellfire's arm, but Hellfire's men returned a hail of gunfire that wheeled him to the floor.

Repeated gunfire made the body twitch and dance as if it were still alive while Hellfire's men gibbered with delight. Only when they'd spent their bullets did they stop. A shroud of gunsmoke hung in the air, the acrid taint making Cooper's eyes water, as Hellfire turned and aimed his gun at Cooper's forehead.

"Now where is Shelton?" he said.

Cooper gulped. "You've just got to believe me. I don't know nothing about him."

Hellfire gestured and the man holding Cooper folded him over the counter.

"Then listen to this." Hellfire gestured to the man on his left, who grabbed Cooper's wrist and thrust his hand flat to the counter. "Talk to me. If I like what I hear, I leave. If I don't like what I hear, I do this."

Hellfire placed the barrel of his gun over Cooper's smallest finger. Cooper tried to flinch away, but the man holding his hand had a grip of iron. Cooper babbled, begging Hellfire not to do anything.

Then Hellfire fired and hot fire ripped into Cooper's finger. He closed his eyes, his back rigid as he steeled himself for the pain. When it didn't come with the intensity he expected he opened his eyes, hoping that maybe nothing had happened. The sight of the blackened stump of his finger made him swing his head to the side and vomit down the side of the bar.

"Now talk before I run out of bits to shoot off you," Hellfire said, slamming the barrel over Cooper's second finger.

* * *

"Do you reckon you'll be able to keep this Hellfire away?" Harvey Baez asked.

The leader of Shelton's hired guns, Eli Payton, raised a foot on to the bottom rail of the corral fence and leaned on his knee.

"The likes of Hellfire don't worry me," he said and spat to the side.

The week since Eli, Garth and Jackson had arrived at the trading post had been fraught for Harvey. Shelton had been permanently on edge, barking commands and always waiting for Hellfire's arrival.

Harvey had bitten his lip to avoid asking the questions he'd wanted to ask and which he knew Shelton didn't want to answer. Instead, he had carried out his duties quietly and spent whatever free time he had observing the sullen new arrivals.

These men had devoted themselves to silent contemplation of the approaching trail, filling the long hours in cleaning their guns with the studious attention of men who rely on their weapons to keep them alive. Harvey had tried to find something to talk to them about, but his failed efforts only went to prove that a young assistant in a trading post had nothing in common with men who killed for a living.

"What will you do when he comes?" Harvey asked.

Eli provided a wink which was so slight that Harvey thought it might have been a tick.

"What we have to do."

Harvey nodded. "And what's that?"

"Boy, you ask too many questions."

Harvey rocked from foot to foot as he searched for something else to say. When he couldn't think of anything, he turned and left Eli, but as he passed Garth, Garth grabbed Harvey's jacket, halting him, and raised it high. He patted his hip and then dropped the jacket.

"Are you not packing a gun yourself?" he asked.

"I can fire one, but my uncle doesn't want me to learn that way of life."

"A man's still got to protect himself." Garth released the coat. "Shelton's not your pa, then?"

"No. My parents died in Calamity's station fire."

Garth nodded, a flash of sympathy appearing in his cold eyes.

"It sounds like you've got a mighty powerful reason to want Hellfire dead for yourself."

Harvey opened his mouth to try to sum up a lifetime of wondering what he'd do if he ever met Hellfire, but from the post doorway, Shelton called for him.

"I've told you before, I don't want you talking to those men," Shelton said as Harvey joined him.

"I was just being friendly."

"I'm sure you were, but these aren't

friendly times and they aren't friendly people." Shelton patted Harvey's shoulder and softened his voice. "Just don't annoy them while they're working."

Harvey nodded and scuffed his feet from side to side as he searched for a way to ask the question he'd wanted to ask ever since these men had arrived.

"When they've finished working are we moving on?" he said.

"What do you mean?"

Harvey sighed. "You promised Eli a whole heap of money, but you haven't got that much money, and I thought that might mean you'll have to sell up."

A smile twitched Shelton's mouth. "Don't worry yourself. We're going nowhere."

"I *am* worried. You've always said this post will be mine one day, and I've often tried to work out how it makes money to pay for our keep, but I can't. So I can't see how you can afford to pay for hired guns."

Shelton breathed deeply through his nostrils, his face reddening to take on a color that was deeper than Harvey had ever seen.

"That's enough, Harvey," he snapped. "It isn't your place to worry about things like that."

"I'll try, uncle." Harvey forced himself to smile. He turned and faced the rocky outcrop on the ridge.

"Stop panicking," Shelton said, the anger gone from his voice. He laid a friendly hand on Harvey's shoulder. "Perhaps I was wrong and Hellfire won't come, after all."

"Perhaps he won't." Harvey shrugged. "But it doesn't stop me looking."

"You've done nothing but look for Hellfire for the last week. Don't think I don't notice."

Harvey kicked at the dirt, wondering whether to raise his second most important question, but on noting the redness that still marred Shelton's face he just nodded and kept quiet. Last week, he'd seen his mother's ghost again.

He'd first seen her as a child, but Shelton had told him it was just a rag caught on a tree, and sure enough, it didn't reappear the next night. Harvey knew what he'd seen and whenever he was in distress, at sundown she'd be standing on the outcrop, facing the trading post, her form silent and enigmatic, but strangely comforting.

Years had passed since he'd last been seriously worried, the nightmares of infernos that had plagued his childhood having departed, but with the arrival of the hired guns, he'd been comforted to see her again. He was sure that mentioning this sighting would result in the ghost leaving again and, in these troubled times, he couldn't face that.

So, to avoid Shelton picking up on his thoughts, he faced down the trail. He flinched and couldn't stop himself emitting a barked screech. At least a dozen riders were heading for the post. Eli and his associates were already watching them with interest.

"Someone's a-coming," he said.

Shelton shivered and, with a pronounced gulp, he turned to the approaching riders.

Harvey opened his mouth to ask if Hellfire were among them, but Shelton's wide-eyed expression made him close his mouth instead.

FOUR

Stark Pass was silent as Lincoln led his men into town. The saloon had a broken window and a notice outside reported that it was closed until further notice. Several stores had closed shutters and the town presented none of the bustling atmosphere that Lincoln had heard it possessed.

At the town marshal's office he dismounted. With his deputies trailing behind, he headed across the boardwalk and backhanded the office door open.

"Marshal Cooper," he said, his voice echoing.

Inside, the marshal was pacing back and forth, cradling a bandaged hand, but he turned to the advancing Lincoln.

"Who wants him?" he asked, his voice shaking as he backed away.

Two paces in from the doorway Lincoln stopped and placed his hands on his hips.

"I'm U.S. Marshal Lincoln Hawk."

Cooper blinked hard. He backed away for another pace and pointed his bandaged hand at him.

"What. . . ? Where. . . ?"

"I haven't got time to waste on questions. A prisoner known as Hellfire has escaped. My guess is he's searching for the fifty thousand dollars that got away, and to cause as much trouble as he can. I intend to give it to him before he gives it to anyone else."

Lincoln withdrew the notice of Hellfire's escape from his pocket and held it out to the marshal, but Cooper didn't even look at it.

"I . . . I don't want to get involved in anything like that."

Lincoln advanced a long pace on Cooper. "You don't? What kind of sorry-assed lawman are you?"

Cooper gulped and shuffled sideways to

his desk with his head down.

"I'm the kind that runs this town, and you don't. Now, leave me alone."

Daniel snorted and Alvin raised an eyebrow.

"I'm not going nowhere, and I'm sure the citizens of Stark Pass will appreciate having some real lawmen in town, but Shelton Baez will be in danger first. He runs a trading post and I'll head out there to check on him." Lincoln sneered. "You can come along if you promise not to get in my way."

Cooper raised his head and pointed a trembling finger at him, the action shaking a globule of blood from his bandaged hand.

"This is my town and this is my—"

"Yeah, yeah, and it will be again when I've left, but maybe after a few days with me, you'll learn how to act like a lawman."

As Cooper lowered his head and muttered to himself, Daniel directed Lincoln to come to the window. Lincoln joined him. Outside five men were striding toward the office, and every one of them had the look of a hired gun.

* * *

Shelton dragged Harvey into the trading post, but Eli hurried after him and slammed a hand on Shelton's shoulder, halting him.

"We came to stop Hellfire, not this many men," he said.

"He must have hired as many guns as he could find." Shelton narrowed his eyes. "You can't mean to leave us."

"I'm not staying around to face that many." Eli turned and barked orders to his associates, Garth and Jackson, to move on out.

"I'll double the payment." Shelton waited, but Eli only paused before carrying on. "All right, I'll treble it."

Garth and Jackson both nodded. As Shelton sighed with relief, Garth took up a position in a hollow beside the corral. Jackson hurried inside and stood by the window. Eli encouraged Shelton to hide, but

Shelton shook his head and collected the gun he kept beneath the counter.

He was a poor aim and a slow draw, but at short distances when his back was to the wall, he claimed he was as deadly as any man was. Harvey nudged Shelton, his eyes bright.

"Uncle, you've got a spare gun," he said.

"I never taught you the way of the gun," Shelton said. "This isn't the time to start."

Harvey murmured his disagreement, but Shelton busied himself with loading the gun and ignored his complaints. Then he ordered Harvey to kneel down behind the counter and, when Harvey complied, he joined Eli by the door.

Despite Shelton's orders Harvey edged back and forth behind the counter until he found a position that let him see through the window. Outside, the riders pulled up twenty yards before the corral. As they spread out Shelton pointed out the rider with a red mark on the face.

"Get that one and the rest will fall apart,"

he said.

As Eli nodded, that man, Hellfire, edged his horse forward.

"Shelton Baez, come on out," he shouted.

"I'm not," Shelton shouted. "Now, just leave me alone."

Hellfire leaned forward in the saddle and chuckled.

"I've waited sixteen years for this. I'm not leaving without your hide."

"Then you'll die here, like you should have done in Calamity."

"The only person dying here is you, except it'll be a long and painful journey."

Hellfire spat to the side. Then he sat back and directed his men to surround the post. Inside, Shelton nodded to Eli and his hired guns blasted a sustained volley of gunfire at Hellfire's men.

The first burst forced Hellfire to dismount in a hurry and scurry with his head down for the nearest cover, Shelton's buckboard. Two of his men weren't so fast and Eli's deadly aim blasted them from their horses, but when the gunshot echoes faded, the bulk of Hellfire's men had gained cover.

Then they started a persistent bombardment of the post. When one volley ended the next began, letting neither Eli nor Jackson return anything more than sporadic retorts. More than one shot ripped through the door and window and, with slugs tearing through the wooden walls, sparks of light spread across the pitted walls.

When one shot whistled across the post and broke a jug on the shelf above Harvey's head, Harvey threw himself to the floor and cowered behind the counter. Then, in disgust at himself, he fast-crawled into the storeroom.

He rummaged beneath a folded pile of cloth and a greased sheet of paper before emerging with the gun Shelton had told him not to use. With the gun held close to his cheek he crawled across the floor and joined Shelton, who gave a reluctant nod, although he did order him to stay away from the window.

Then three of Hellfire's men ran for the door. By the window, Jackson slammed a slug into one of the men's arms, which wheeled him to the ground. Outside, Garth leaped up to rip gunfire into the other man.

The second man went down, but the third man blasted lead into Garth's guts, forcing him to stagger back. Before he could right himself the wounded man tore lead into his chest from the ground.

Then he and a line of men ran to the post to press themselves to the wall and out of Harvey's view through the door. The outlines of the men were visible through gaps in the slats, so Harvey ventured out from the counter and fired, aiming to shoot them in the back through the wall.

The shots were wild, but it did have the effect of forcing them away from the wall. From the window Jackson fired, knocking one of these men to the ground, killing him instantly. Then he ripped gunfire into the second man's stomach, but, with a dying blast through the window, this man hammered a slug into Jackson's neck which made him stumble away from the window.

Eli turned to Jackson as a stray bullet from outside tore into his shoulder forcing him to back into the post. A cry of triumph came from outside and footfalls pattered as Hellfire's men advanced on the post.

Shelton darted into the doorway and fired two quick and desperate shots, but when a hail of gunfire exploded, sending splinters from the wood cascading around him, he bleated and took hold of Harvey's arm. He dragged him back to the counter and, with the wounded Eli, they spread out, ready to make their last stand.

Outside, Hellfire shouted taunts, his men whooping their delight as they made their group sound as if it were twice the size while they fanned out in front of the post door. Eli winced and directed a slow shake of the head at Shelton.

"Harvey, it's time for you to hide," Shelton said, his voice low and urgent. "Head to the dug-out and no matter what you hear, don't come out."

"I won't run," Harvey said.

He kneeled behind the counter and placed both hands on the top, the gun held between them. He aimed at the door ready to take the first man who ventured through.

"You will," Shelton said, considering Harvey's shaking hands. "This is not your problem and you have to live to do something for me."

Shelton reached under the counter and removed a wooden box, about six inches long and three inches high. Harvey reckoned he'd seen everything in the post, but he'd never seen this small box before.

"What—?"

Shelton raised a hand, silencing him, and then pushed the box down the counter until it nudged Harvey's hand.

"Get this to . . . get this to her."

Harvey took the box and fingered the plain sides, but then Shelton's comment filtered through to his mind.

"To *her*?"

Shelton's eyes watered, but whether with an old memory or fear of what would happen, Harvey couldn't tell.

"You know, Harvey, you know."

Harvey threw himself into Shelton's arms and held on.

"Whatever happens, I want you to know that even though you weren't my real father, you brought me up real—"

"You've got nothing you need to say to me." A burst of gunfire tore through the window, forcing them both to duck. On his knees, Shelton pointed to the storeroom. "Now, go!"

Still Harvey wavered, but Shelton turned his back on him and hunkered down, the gun resting on the counter. Harvey risked bobbing up to grab the box and thrust it in his pocket. He scurried into the storeroom and when he reached the back exit, he threw open the door, but then skidded to a halt.

A shadow lay across the entrance. Hellfire was blocking his way.

FIVE

As the hired guns approached the law office, Lincoln turned from the window to face Marshal Cooper.

"Do you know anything about these men?" he asked.

"No, and I don't take kindly to lawmen riding into my town and asking me questions," Cooper said, ignoring the hired guns.

"Then, Marshal, I'll tell you what I think." Lincoln beckoned for Cooper to join him at the window. He drew his gun. "Hellfire is in search of a whole heap of money and news like that attracts hired guns. I'll have to explain to them why they've made a big mistake."

Cooper sneered. "You're just plain trouble,

Lincoln."

"I sure am, and I reckon you'll learn plenty about being a lawman in the next two minutes." Lincoln directed Daniel to take a position beside the door. "Just keep your head down and you might live for long enough to use it."

"All right," Cooper screeched, his eyes watering. "They are with Hellfire and you can't let them know who you are. Just go while you still can and leave the talking to me."

Lincoln snorted, as the sprawl of hired guns outside bunched up to murmur to each other in front of the office. A ripple of nodding passed between them and then they ran for cover to take up positions in the alleyway beside the law office and behind the barrels in front of the store on the opposite side of the main drag.

"You men heard right," Lincoln shouted after them. "Marshal Lincoln Hawk is in town and if you reckon you're tough enough you'd better head in here and get me, but it'll be the last thing you'll do."

"You'll regret that taunt," a man shouted from behind one of the barrels.

Lincoln gestured at Alvin and Daniel, conveying his orders silently, but as his deputies took up their positions, Cooper slapped a hand on his shoulder and dragged him around. Cooper's eyes were beseeching and when he spoke, his voice was gruff and defeated.

"Don't take them on, Lincoln," he said.

Lincoln shook his head. "I don't let outlaws dictate to me."

"I do."

"If that's *your* policy in *your* town, I'm not having nothing to do with it."

"You will when Hellfire's kidnapped my family." Cooper rubbed his eyes with the back of his bandaged hand. "If I don't hand you over to those men outside, he'll kill my wife and children."

* * *

Harvey threw the door closed with sufficient force to bundle Hellfire on to his back and then turned around. As Hellfire cursed, Harvey scampered through the storeroom. Behind him, the door crashed open, but then he skidded to a halt.

In the main room Shelton and Eli were making their last stand, but Hellfire's men were becoming bolder as they alternated between firing through the window and door. Their gunfire exploded across the post, ripping splinters from the counter and forcing Shelton and Eli to dive for cover.

Harvey wondered how he could prevail against such sustained fire, but the gun fell from his sweat-slickened hand and landed beside a double-doored cabinet. He moved to get it, but the creeping fear that was numbing his mind had enforced clumsiness upon him and he banged his head on one of the doors.

Behind him, Hellfire was stomping closer. In desperation Harvey threw open the nearest door and leaped inside to hide in the corner. The door swung closed, as gunfire blazed across the post.

A stray bullet ripped through the wood a foot above Harvey's head, forcing him to cringe himself into the smallest ball he could make. Through the sliver of action he could see, he saw a bullet hammer into Eli's chest, splaying his body over the counter.

Eli rolled from the counter, staggered a pace and then fell, slamming into the cabinet and splintering the wood. The piece of furniture rocked and came crashing down, landing on its front and half over his body.

Harvey flattened his hands over his ears, muffling the barked commands for Shelton to give himself up, but from the tone of Shelton's oath-filled replies, Harvey reckoned he'd fight to the last.

Then Hellfire's men stormed the post. Bullets flew everywhere, at least three thudding into Eli's body. Trapped in the cabinet, Harvey had no choice but to keep still and hope. Beyond the broken door Eli lay in a pool of spreading blood.

"I've got you trapped, Shelton," Hellfire said.

"I'm not coming out, Hellfire," Shelton said. "I'll die before I surrender to you."

A snort sounded. "You haven't got the guts to fight to the death."

Footfalls pounded across the post and then the sound of two men crashing together. A gunshot blasted and then grunts and scuffing feet suggested a tussle. Hellfire uttered a cry of triumph.

"Get your hands off me," Shelton whimpered.

Hellfire snorted. "I *was* right. You haven't got the courage to die." A slap sounded and then the sound of a body hitting the floor. "Now, where's the other one?"

"What other one?" someone asked.

"This runt tried to escape. He went back into the post. Find him!"

Thuds sounded as Hellfire's men tipped crates over and hurled boxes around the room. The clutter in the post was considerable, but Harvey held out no hope that they wouldn't find him.

Moving as quietly as he could, he squee-zed his hand through the gap in the door, feeling Eli's body beneath the doors and searching for his gun. He felt only dampness and he was thankful that in the poor light, he couldn't see what he'd touched.

He listened to each crate falling, mentally picturing their progress around the post. They were coming closer. The cabinet shook as a man tried to lift it. Harvey held his breath, hoping that the man would consider the fallen piece of furniture as being somewhere he wouldn't hide.

The man called for another, Burl, to join him and, with a surge, they righted the cabinet. The doors clattered open and then shut, but they were open long enough to reveal Harvey. Forlornly, Harvey cringed into the corner, but Hellfire threw open the doors and grinned at him. Then Burl's rough hands bundled him out and stood him straight.

"What are you going to do with me?"

Harvey said, although he saw no hope of mercy in Hellfire's blemished face and blank eyes.

Hellfire snorted and turned to Shelton. "Is this your son, Shelton?"

Shelton set his jaw firm, his eyes displaying a coldness that Harvey knew was false.

"He isn't mine."

"Then it won't concern you when I kill him." Hellfire raised his gun and sighted Harvey's chest.

Harvey struggled, but on finding that Burl was holding him securely from the side, he puffed his chest.

"He doesn't deserve to die," Shelton said. "He's done nothing to you."

"He hasn't." Hellfire fingered his chin, a smile emerging. "But I can see in your eyes that you have a connection to him."

"It's called humanity. Something you know nothing about."

"You're wrong there, but you have ten seconds to tell me about the fifty thousand dollars that went missing." Hellfire licked his lips. "Or I'll kill him."

Shelton gulped. "I know nothing about that. I was in the station getting nearly burned to death with the rest of your other victims."

"Except you got out alive, and I reckon you know what happened to that money." Hellfire roved his gun in a circle, aiming at Harvey's head, and then chest, and then head again. "If I'm wrong, it'll cost you this young man's life."

Shelton gulped, his breath coming short and hard. "If you want to know what happened back at that station, ask Marshal Billy Epstein. He's retired now, but that man was as useless as any lawman I've ever met and if someone spirited that money away, it was him."

"Marshal Epstein," Hellfire mused.

When his men gave a variety of snorts and muttered comments, Hellfire clicked his fingers. A grunted series of orders passed between Hellfire's men before being relayed outside.

With Hellfire facing the door, Harvey turned and winced when Billy Epstein paced into the post. Billy snarled, and when he reached Shelton he backhanded his cheek, rocking his head to the side. Hellfire chuckled and turned to Harvey.

"If Shelton won't plead for your life, will you?" he demanded.

"Never," Harvey said. He firmed his jaw and coughed to eliminate the tremor in his voice. "I've forgiven you for what you did to me a long time ago."

Hellfire's right eye twitched. "Forgiven me?"

"You burned down Calamity's station and killed my—"

"I didn't burn down that station and I lost more than. . . ." Hellfire snorted. Then he lowered his head, a maniacal gleam in his eye. "I'm afraid you won't be so lucky today. You get to live."

He barked an order to Burl and, with Billy's help, they bundled him into a chair. Harvey struggled, but they clamped firm hands on his shoulders and secured him to the chair with thick bonds.

When they stood back, Harvey tried to catch Shelton's eye, but Hellfire pushed his head to the side and forced him to face the back of the post. A chuckle sounded.

"No!" Shelton cried, but a sharp slap echoed across the post. Then Hellfire dragged him outside, Shelton screeching and pleading at every pace.

Behind Harvey, Hellfire's men scampered out after him while Burl stayed in the post. Harvey strained his hearing, wondering what he was doing, but as far as he could tell he just pattered around the post.

The back of Harvey's neck burned as he anticipated whatever Burl was going to do to him, but deep in the pit of his stomach a faint hope burgeoned that he would leave him alive. Then the door slammed shut.

Scraping and thudding sounded, as of someone placing a barrier across the door. With a long breath held deep in his chest, Harvey tensed, listening and confirming that he was now alone, although Hellfire's men were still moving around outside.

Harvey closed his eyes and took a deep breath, trying to gulp down the fear that had clamped his throat. Then a crackle sounded. Harvey forced his head to turn as far as it would go. Part of the floor was well-lit, far more than the interior darkness should allow.

That light flickered and, with a flash of shocked heat, he realized what was happening. Hellfire was torching the post.

* * *

"So if these men reckon you're helping me, Hellfire will kill your family?" Lincoln said.

Cooper wrung his bandaged hand. "That's the way it is."

"Then I guess you'd better stay out of this."

Lincoln turned away, but then turned back, his fist snapping up to connect with Cooper's jaw and send him reeling into his desk. The marshal folded over the desk to lie sprawled on the other side.

Lincoln ensured he was out cold and then turned to the office window. One of the hired guns jumped up from behind a barrel and blasted at the office, the lead winging through the window and sending glass flying.

Lincoln ducked and waited for the barrage to end, and then bobbed up. The hired gun was still standing, so he fired a slug through the broken window. With deadly accuracy, it ripped into the man's chest and slammed him back against the wall.

A second slug to the head whirled him around to lie sprawled over the barrel with his arms dangling. Quiet descended. Lincoln pressed himself flat to the wall, but none of the other hired guns were visible outside.

"Perhaps they're trying to outflank us," Alvin said with a shrug.

"Or perhaps they got sense and ran," Daniel said from the other side of the window.

Lincoln shrugged. "Or they might have gone to fetch reinforcements."

As Alvin and Daniel winced Lincoln gestured to them, delivering orders that didn't require words. He counted to three on raised fingers. Then the lawmen hurried from the office with their guns brandished.

Alvin went left, Daniel went right and Lincoln headed straight forward. Daniel and Alvin hunkered down, covering both sides of town. Then, down the alleyway, a gun protruded. Lincoln blasted a shot at the gun, ripping shards from the wall and forcing the man to back into the alleyway. Then two men came into view on the law office roof.

"On high," Lincoln shouted.

On their knees, Alvin and Daniel turned and fired up at the roof. Alvin hit the first man in the chest, the man tumbling forward over the false-front to slam into the dirt beside him, but the second man got in a wild shot that ripped past Lincoln's leg.

Lincoln steadied his aim and fired, knocking the man back. As the man stood straight with the blow, both Daniel and Alvin hammered gunfire into him which crashed him on to his back before he slid from the roof and thudded to the boardwalk.

Lincoln counted through their successes, but even as he decided two more men remained, Alvin and Daniel blasted a volley of shots behind him. He turned as a man fell backward through the store window, his hands clutching his reddening chest, and that just left the man in the alleyway.

Lincoln gestured with his hands facing down, signifying that they would try to take this man alive, and then hurried to the side of the alleyway. There he waited, and sure enough, the gun slipped out from the alleyway.

The man fired, but Lincoln aimed at the gun, winging it from his grasp. The force dragged the man's arm out from the alleyway and Lincoln lunged for that arm, and then yanked him out on to the boardwalk.

He gained a firmer grip. Then he stood him straight and slugged his jaw. The man crashed on to his back, but Lincoln was on him in an instant. He grabbed his collar, pulled him high and slammed his gun barrel between his eyes.

"Mortimer T. Foster, I never thought I'd see your ugly hide again," he said.

"Hellfire will make you pay for this," Mortimer snarled.

"I don't think so. Now, do you want me to blast you away, or will you take me to Hellfire?"

"I guess you'll just have to kill me. I'm not double-crossing Hellfire."

"Then maybe I'll just. . . ." Lincoln firmed his gun hand, his finger tightening the trigger. Then, with a grin, Lincoln lowered his gun. "I'll just let you go."

"Lincoln," Alvin said.

"Don't worry." Lincoln dragged Mortimer to his feet and stood him straight. "Mortimer is going to deliver a message to Hellfire."

"What's the message?" Mortimer said, hope alighting in his eyes despite his arrogance.

"Tell Hellfire this is between him and me. It always was and it always will be. Tell him there's only one place we could ever meet to end this, and I'll expect him there at sundown."

"Where's that?"

Lincoln swung Mortimer around and kicked his rump, knocking him forward.

"Hellfire knows."

SIX

Harvey struggled, but the thick bonds around his wrists meant he couldn't move his hands. The fire was licking at the crates and rising ever higher toward the ceiling. It would be only minutes before the post was an inferno.

With a growing emptiness in his stomach he struggled against his bonds, but they were tight. For a second he closed his eyes to force calm. Hellfire's men had tied his legs together and his hands behind his back.

Although they had secured his hands to the chair, they hadn't bound his feet to the chair legs. Harvey rocked back and forth, and then mustered a huge push that rolled him to his feet.

He steadied himself and hopped forward. Ignoring the bloodied and heaped bodies of the gunslingers whom Shelton and Eli had dispatched, he shuffled across the post to the door and leaned against it, but the door didn't move.

He hammered against the door with his shoulders, but couldn't move the solid wood and whatever obstruction Hellfire had placed over the door. With a terrible burst of fear dampening his brow and making his heart race, he slumped back into the chair and thrust his legs up at the door.

He strained, pushing his legs forward. The door creaked, but it didn't move. He rejected this escape method and rocked to his feet. Then he shuffled around to face away from the door and leaped backward.

The chair cut into his legs and his hands dug deep into the small of his back, but he ignored the pain and repeated the action. This time, a crack sounded and the chair partially collapsed beneath him.

Not holding back this time, he leaped at

the door and the chair collapsed into fire-wood beneath him. Although unencumbered by the chair, his arms and thighs were still bound.

Flames licked at the ceiling, which blackened and shrank from the blaze. With pained coughs racking his chest, Harvey abandoned his attempt to batter down the door. Fire had already blocked his route to the back exit so he shuffled to the window instead.

Without time to work out how to rip the rope from his thighs, he threw himself against the wooden shutters, but they held as fast as the door did. The ceiling was reddening. Motes of black soot cascaded down.

He blinked to clear his watering eyes, but cloying smoke was fogging his vision. Through his watering eyes he noted the circles of light that the sustained gunfire had ripped into the wooden walls, and in one plank several holes were close together.

In desperation Harvey hurled his shoulder at this spot. A crack sounded deep within the wood and he hurled himself again. It may have been his imagination, but this time he was sure the wall gave a little.

He slammed his shoulder against the wall again and another crack sounded, but it was no louder than before, so Harvey searched around on the floor. The only object he found that might help him break out was a poker.

He kneeled and rolled on to his back. The poker stuck into the small of his back. Desperate seconds passed as he tried to wiggle it into his hands. Above him, the roof was alight. Waves of flame rippled along the underside.

Flurries of soot rained down in burning flakes. The heat grew by the moment, drying his sweat and baking his face. He gave a cry of relief as the poker slipped into his hands. He rolled to his feet.

As the smoke burned his throat he gulped, but the effort didn't help his parched throat. He shook his head to free a growing desire to sleep and bounded to the wall, turned and maneuvered the poker between two planks.

With a wrenching tug, he spun away. Wood splintered and pulled away. Wasting no time, Harvey raised the poker higher and repeated the action. Another strip of wood splintered, but the remainder of the plank was solid and it was higher than he could raise his bound hands.

Harvey dropped the poker and rolled to the ground. He wriggled, forcing his hands to the back of his heels and then dragged them beneath his boots to his front. With more freedom of movement he picked up the poker and yanked along the plank, levering away whole sections of wood.

When he'd cleared a one-yard length he started on the plank below. With the additional leverage afforded by the gap he was able to splinter the wood away. He coughed as an intense wave of heat rippled across his back.

He was sure he could feel blisters breaking out, but he gritted his teeth and con-centrated on the plank. Then behind him, a crash sounded as the roof collapsed. Half-blinded by the thickening smoke, he put all his strength into one muscle-ripping pull.

In an explosion of splinters, he dragged away the next plank. Behind him, the heat was intense, burning his back and singeing his clothes. With no choice, he thrust his head through the gap.

It looked too small to slip through but, with one last desperate shove, he forced his shoulders through, ripping out more wood as he half-threw, half-fell through the gap to freedom. While Harvey floundered on the ground outside, dragging in cooling gasps of air, a plume of smoke exploded through the hole as the ceiling collapsed.

Then he remembered that Hellfire could still be outside. Coughing so badly he thought he'd be ill, he groped on the ground and picked up the poker. He stood defiant, waiting for Hellfire to try to force him inside.

He waited, but only the occasional bird-call greeted him and the plains were as peaceful as they had been before Hellfire arrived, but then something moved to his side. Harvey turned and, as he'd half-expected, the caped figure was standing on the rocky outcrop.

Despite everything, Harvey smiled to himself. Then he walked toward the figure.

* * *

The outlaw Mortimer Foster edged away from Lincoln, his uncertain steps suggesting he couldn't believe that Lincoln would really let him go. Lincoln gave an encouraging nod and he darted back, and then scurried for his horse.

He mounted his steed and headed away, but as he gained open land on the edge of town, a bullet ripped out and tore into Mortimer's side, knocking him sideways. Marshal Cooper had regained consciousness and now stood in the office doorway, his gun drawn and smoking.

Lincoln thrust up his arm to grab the

marshal's arm and send his second shot high in the air, and then turned around. Mortimer slipped from his saddle. One foot became caught in a stirrup. He was dragged after his horse and, as he bounded out of town without attempting to regain the saddle, Lincoln reckoned he was dead.

"Why did you do that?" Lincoln demanded.

"He was getting away," Cooper said.

"I wanted him to. I'd thrown down my challenge to Hellfire."

"It's not your place to do that. This isn't your investigation."

"It isn't, but how did killing that man help?"

Cooper felt his jaw as he walked out on to the boardwalk.

"Knocking me out to keep me away from the fight wouldn't convince that man I wasn't helping you. So he would have reported what he saw to Hellfire and he'd have killed my family, just as he'd threatened to."

Lincoln snorted a breath through his

nostrils, but then gave a begrudging nod and let Cooper return to his office. He gestured for his deputies to follow him in, but he waited for the townsfolk to come out of hiding for the first time since he'd returned to Stark Pass.

He gestured to them in a placating way to let them know this crisis was over. Several people gestured back at him and Lincoln was pleased to recognize many of them from his previous time in the area, but among the faces there was one man he wasn't pleased to see.

Marshal Billy Epstein was alone outside the saloon, mounted on a horse which, from its sweating flanks, Lincoln reckoned he'd just ridden into town. Even if his wizened form suggested he'd ceased to be a lawman for some years, Lincoln still had nothing but contempt for him after his role in the events of sixteen years ago.

From Billy's sneer and the way he snapped the reins around and rode out of town, he guessed the feeling was mutual. When Billy swung around the last buildings on the edge of town, heading north, Lincoln turned to the law office.

"North," he said to himself, the hint of a long-forgotten memory tapping at his thoughts. "There isn't nothing north of Stark Pass worth visiting except the caves in Wildman's Gulch."

SEVEN

"Are you ready to talk?" Hellfire asked as he walked toward the cringing Shelton.

With a hand raised to fend off any blows, Shelton back-kicked along the ground until he banged his head against the cave wall. He faced Hellfire and his twenty or so men, their eager grins showing no hint of mercy.

In their midst were three other hostages: Leah Cooper and her two children. Shelton hoped he might share a moment of compassion with another decent person, but they ignored him. At his side was a cage, about six-foot high and four-foot square, the bars solid iron. Shelton tried to ignore the heavy lock on the door and the manacles dangling from the top.

"I haven't got nothing to say to you, Hellfire," he said.

"Now that isn't friendly," Hellfire said, pouting his bottom lip with mock indignation.

"Quit mocking me and tell me what you want."

"I want you to talk. Then I want you to die." Hellfire pointed at the cage and grinned. "I'll get that wish soon."

Shelton gulped to moisten his drying throat.

"What are you going to do?" he said and then bit his bottom lip in irritation at voicing his fear.

"I haven't decided." With his movements steady, Hellfire drew a knife from his boot. "It depends on how quickly you talk. Fifty thousand dollars went missing. It should have been on the train, but it wasn't and I have it on good authority that you know where that money went."

"Billy Epstein wasn't a reliable source of information sixteen years ago and he isn't now."

"I know that." Hellfire slammed his boot to the cave wall beside Shelton's face and leaned on his knee. "I trust my methods of making people talk, and I reckon I can make you suffer the equivalent of sixteen years of prison in one day."

"You didn't go to prison because of me. You went for all the trouble you caused in Calamity."

"Without you speaking up, that wouldn't have happened." Hellfire stabbed his knife at the cave wall. A flurry of grit escaped to cascade on to Shelton's head. "I've heard it said that you can keep a man alive for days, making a nick here and a nick there."

Hellfire continued to stab at the wall, his actions becoming stronger, but then he hurled the knife away for it to stab into the dirt.

"Or then again, I might do something even worse," he continued, noting the fire in the cave entrance.

"Hellfire, you have to believe me. I was

with you when you torched . . ." Shelton gulped. ". . . when that fire broke out. I know nothing about the fifty thousand dollars. I know nothing about nothing."

Hellfire lowered his leg to the ground and stepped back.

"Are you calling the death of my woman – Adele – nothing?"

Shelton furrowed his brow. "You mean that whore you kidnapped and—"

"That was no whore!" Hellfire roared, spit flying from his mouth to splatter Shelton's face. "She was a fine woman."

A nervous giggle broke out from one of Hellfire's men and Hellfire swirled around to confront him.

"What are you laughing at?" he demanded, his voice echoing in the cave.

The man searched everyone's eyes, perhaps for support, but receiving nothing but sad shakes of the head and an almost imperceptible shuffling away from him to leave him standing alone.

"Nothing," he said with his head lowered.

"Then what were you laughing at?"

"I guess Shelton was right." He took a deep breath. "From what I've heard Adele wasn't exactly—"

Hellfire roared with anger and stormed across the cave. The man backed away, throwing his hands in front of his face, but Hellfire still lunged and grabbed his throat. He marched him to the cave wall and, with his back braced, raised him from the ground.

The man struggled, but Hellfire had secured a firm grip of his throat and held him against the wall. The man battered Hellfire's fists, his face darkening and the blows landing with reducing force. His eyes boggled, but nobody moved to help him and Hellfire just dragged him higher up the cave wall until his arm was fully outstretched.

"Tell me about Adele. Tell me she was a fine woman. Tell me!"

The man battered at Hellfire's arms, but his grip was so tight that the blood had drained from the knuckles. He opened his mouth and only a pained screech emerged, along with his lolling tongue.

"I said, tell me!" Hellfire roared.

Hellfire thrust up his arm to its utmost and, with a last bubbling moan, the man went limp. Hellfire still held on for another minute, his head cocked to one side and still demanding that he answer him.

Then he snorted and hurled the limp body away. It landed in a crumpled heap as Hellfire batted his hands together. Then he stepped over it and confronted his huddle of men.

"Anyone else got anything to say about my woman?"

As Hellfire's men avoided catching his eye, Shelton shuffled into the base of the cave wall. He tried to make his form as small as possible in the forlorn hope that maybe this distraction would keep Hellfire from noticing him.

Almost as if he *had* forgotten, Hellfire strode away from him and through the parting group of men to stand over his other hostages. The firelight from the front of the cave illuminated Hellfire's smile, all signs of his former raging anger fading as he hunkered down before Leah.

"How are you?" he said.

Leah clutched the two children closer to her chest.

"We'll be fine as soon as you release us," she said, a tremor in her voice despite her defiance.

"I'm not doing that until your husband's finished helping me." Hellfire reached out to finger a lock of the elder child's hair. "Which he will if he wants to see these charming children again."

"Stay away from her," Leah said.

"Relax. I wouldn't hurt a child." Hellfire leaned down and brushed the curl to the side. "What's your name, little one?"

"I'm Mollie," the girl said, her voice small and frightened.

"You're not scared of me, are you?"

Mollie shrugged. "No, I guess."

"You guess? You don't sound sure. How

can I persuade you I'm a nice man?"

"Letting us go would help," Leah said.

Hellfire sneered. Then he softened his expression as he faced Mollie.

"Perhaps we could play a game. That might make you laugh." He winked at Mollie and then clapped his mouth while making silly faces until she giggled and nodded. He clicked his fingers above his head. "Fetch me three mugs."

The man that Shelton reckoned was Hellfire's closest confidant, Burl, dashed to the back of the cave and returned with three mugs. Hellfire set them on the ground before Mollie. Then he reached into his shirt and unhooked a locket from his neck, which he placed beneath the middle mug.

"What's the game?" Mollie asked, her eyes brightening for the first time.

"You have to guess where the locket is. If you do, you'll get to keep it."

Hellfire raised the middle mug to show her that the locket was still there, and then shuffled the mug to the side and around the

86

right-hand mug. Then he took the left-hand mug in his left hand and moved the mugs in a figure-of-eight pattern.

All the time Mollie watched the mug with the locket under it. When Hellfire sat back and raised his hands, she tapped the central mug, but when Hellfire tipped the mug over, there was nothing beneath it.

Mollie knuckled her eyes. "I watched. It has to be there."

"Then you shouldn't have taken the locket." Hellfire winked and reached out to cup her ear. He pulled back to reveal the locket in his hand. "You had it behind your ear all along."

"I was sure it. . . ." She grinned. "Show me again."

Hellfire chuckled. "This time, watch the mugs more closely."

While he shuffled the mugs in a convoluted pattern, in the cave entrance Hellfire's men started muttering to each. Outside, a horse neighed, but Hellfire remained hunched over the mugs, his concentration centered on Mollie's rapt expression as he circled the mugs around each other.

Then fast footfalls pattered and Billy Epstein scurried through the entrance. Burl hailed Hellfire, and Hellfire turned to him, his eyes blazing.

"Don't interrupt me when I'm entertaining my favorite little girl," he said.

"It's that marshal and he doesn't look happy," Burl said.

Hellfire leaned over the mugs, snorting, and then slapped them to the side. His hand whirled as he pocketed the locket. Then he flashed Mollie an apologetic smile and stood up to face the cave entrance, where Billy walked through the milling outlaws to face him.

"What's wrong?" Hellfire asked, his blazing eyes suggesting that the price of a poor answer would be terminal.

"Marshal Lincoln Hawk, that's what wrong," Billy said. "He arrived and took out all the men you left in town. Then he tried to give you a message. He wants to meet you and end this."

"Where?"

"I'd only just arrived back in town when the shooting started. I managed to snoop around in an alleyway. I didn't hear everything he said, but I reckon he said that you'd know."

Hellfire licked his lips and gave a slow nod. "I guess I do. What happened to Marshal Cooper?"

"He killed Mortimer," Billy said. "He's double-crossed you."

Hellfire flared his eyes, but Leah shook her head.

"He wouldn't endanger. . . ." she said, her voice trailing off to shocked silence.

"It would seem he has." Hellfire walked around on the spot to face Leah.

"Don't do anything," she pleaded, cringing.

"I won't harm *you*." Hellfire hunkered down beside the children, a huge smile on his lips. "You enjoyed playing with me, didn't you?"

"Yes, sir," Mollie said.

"Yes, sir," Hellfire said, nodding. "As you're so polite, we could play another game. You say the rhyme – *around and around I go and where my finger stops nobody knows.*" Hellfire pointed at himself and then at Mollie with each word. "When your finger stops, whoever you're pointing at is the winner."

Mollie giggled. Then she started the rhyme.

"Around and around," she said, her small voice loud in the silence that had descended on the cave as she pointed at herself and then at Hellfire.

"I've already played the game," Hellfire said. "This time, play it with your baby sister."

Mollie nodded and restarted the rhyme.

"Around and around I go," she said, her small finger pointing to herself and then at her sister. "And where my finger stops nobody knows."

She chortled and clapped her hands when

she stopped the rhyme with her finger pointing at herself.

"You won," Hellfire said.

Mollie clapped her hands. "What have I won?"

Hellfire just grinned.

* * *

Lincoln knocked back the dregs of his coffee and sat back in his chair. It'd been three hours since the gunfight suggesting his assumption that the skirmish would have attracted a man who could never avoid a confrontation was wrong. Cooper joined him, his eyes downcast, and refilled his coffee.

"I'm obliged." Lincoln regarded the lawman. "I understand your problem, but that won't stop me telling you that you shouldn't have helped Hellfire."

Cooper slumped down on the edge of his desk, his eyes watery and dull.

"I had to. Hellfire gave me no choice."

"You always have a choice." Lincoln leaned forward. "If we work together we can find Hellfire and free your family."

Cooper flexed his bandaged hand. When he spoke, his voice was low.

"All right."

Lincoln softened his expression and lowered his voice.

"Now, tell me everything you know about their capture."

Cooper nodded, but as he opened his mouth, Alvin, from by the window, grunted. Lincoln and Cooper headed across the room as a rider galloped by outside. The rider reached behind him and hurled a package which thudded into the door.

Everyone scurried away from the door, but when thirty seconds had passed and the explosion they'd all feared hadn't materialized, Lincoln headed to the window. The package still lay on the boardwalk.

He opened the door with his gun thrust out, but the man who had hurled the package was already galloping out of town, heading north. Lincoln hefted the package, feeling a heavy and possibly moist object slither around inside a box as he slipped back into the law office. He placed the package on Cooper's desk and moved to open it, but Cooper shooed him away.

"I've had enough of your interfering," he said.

Lincoln backed away across the room. His deputies had raised their eyebrows, but Lincoln just shrugged. With a knife, Cooper slit open the package and raised a corner. He gulped, slammed the lid closed and dropped down into his chair.

His undamaged hand came up to hold his chin, but it was shaking so much he slumped to lie with his face buried in his arms. A sob escaped his lips. Lincoln joined him and, with slow movements, raised a corner of the lid.

He grimaced and let it fall back down. Alvin and Daniel were heading toward him, but Lincoln raised a hand, halting them.

"It's a dead baby," he said.

"That isn't just a baby," Cooper roared, snapping up to confront Lincoln. "That's my child, and Hellfire's gone and hacked it to pieces because I helped you. My child is lying there all mutilated and torn because of you."

"I did nothing that'd—"

"Quit answering back." Cooper leaned forward, raising on his heels to share Lincoln's eyeline, but then he turned around and hammered his undamaged hand on his desk.

"Alvin, get him a whiskey," Lincoln said, his voice low.

Alvin located a bottle of whiskey in a cabinet. He poured a drink and held it out to the marshal. Cooper shrugged away from the glass, but when Lincoln insisted he gulped down half the drink. Then he hurled the glass away for it to smash against the wall.

"I'm not drinking my way out of this."

"I never said you should."

"You did this, Lincoln." Cooper pointed at

the box. "You did this."

"If you think that's true, I'm sorry."

"Sorry isn't good enough. Your gun-toting ways killed her. You rode into my town and you only thought of yourself and your gun and your target. You didn't care about who else suffered."

"I did, believe me. If there was anything I could have done to stop this, I would have, but—"

"I don't want to hear the buts." Cooper pointed at the door, his finger firm. "You'll leave my town now and you won't ever come back."

Lincoln backed away for a short pace, but then stopped and held his hands wide apart.

"You need my help to save the rest of your family."

"I don't." Cooper stormed across the office to stand before Lincoln, his face bright red and his fists raised. "Get out before I kill you with my bare hands!"

EIGHT

"I can't believe we're really leaving," Alvin said as he mounted his horse.

Lincoln set his jaw firm as he led his deputies out of Stark Pass at a steady trot.

"Cooper gave me no choice," he said when they reached the edge of town.

"Yeah, but despite everything, we have the right to—"

"Sometimes right doesn't matter," Lincoln snapped, turning in the saddle. "Cooper's grieving awful bad and we have to leave him."

"Then it seems we really are going," Alvin said.

They rode out of town and headed west. His deputies murmured to each other, but

Lincoln didn't feel inclined to explain his reasoning. He remained silent until they were ten miles out of Stark Pass.

When he was near to cresting a familiar incline before a long ridge he issued orders to his deputies to be on their guard. Before they reached the top of the knoll a plume of smoke rose up ahead.

Lincoln sped his horse down the other side. Within two minutes the blackened skeleton of the building became visible. When he realized that the smoke was the dying remnants of a fire and not a recent happening, he drew his horse to a halt and considered the wrecked trading post. Then he turned to Alvin.

"That's Shelton Baez's trading post." He sighed. "Or at least it used to be."

"It seems Hellfire got there ahead of us." Alvin winced and raised the reins. "We'd better check it out."

"There's no need," Lincoln said. "We don't need to confirm what we'll find there."

Alvin still edged his horse forward, but

then he nodded and turned his back on the post.

"Was Shelton the only surviving witness to what happened in Calamity sixteen years ago?"

"Yeah, aside from me and. . . ." Lincoln sighed. "You both heard what Marshal Cooper said. We've got no right interfering in his investigation, and even if we had, he's got kin at stake and he doesn't want my help."

"We know that," Alvin said.

"I know your views that we should do something anyhow, but you've got to know this isn't about Hellfire and it isn't about Cooper's kin. This is about Hellfire and me, and I can't ask you to join me."

Alvin smiled. "So you are going after Hellfire, after all?"

When Lincoln returned the smile, Daniel and Alvin turned to each other and shrugged. Then they faced Lincoln.

"Then so are we," Daniel said.

Lincoln nodded and, without further

word, swung his horse around. He galloped north, his deputies hurrying to keep up with him. They galloped in an arc around Stark Pass, crossing the railroad tracks five miles out of town.

When they reached the main trail north, Lincoln continued along it until he reached a point where the trail wended a path through a phalanx of boulders. He directed Alvin to take a lookout position on the top of the smallest of the boulders.

Then he and Daniel waited beside a heap of boulders that protected them from the view of anyone riding south. They waited quietly. Both deputies had worked with Lincoln before and they didn't need to ask him what his plan was, trusting that what-ever hunch he was backing would explain itself in due course.

Sure enough, after an hour of patient waiting Alvin waved at Lincoln and raised a finger. Lincoln returned a nod.

"Billy Epstein," he mouthed to Daniel.

The lawmen edged to the side of the trail.

Presently, Billy trotted through the boulders, but on seeing Lincoln he flinched. He moved to turn his horse around and head back north, but Alvin had already jumped down behind him and blocked his way.

While Billy was still undecided as to what to do Lincoln hurried along and blocked his forward route. Daniel grabbed the horse's reins. Billy struggled, trying to tear the reins away, but when Lincoln drew his gun and sighted on his chest, he relented and let Daniel lead his horse toward Lincoln, who smiled at him.

"Billy Epstein, I've been waiting for you," he said.

"I was on business," Billy said. "You've got no right stopping me from going about that business."

"You're right. I've got no right to do nothing." Lincoln holstered his gun. Then he raised his hand and clenched it into a tight fist. "Unless you've broken the law, then I've got every right to drag you off that horse and deal with you."

"I used to be a town marshal. I haven't ever broken no law."

Lincoln raised his eyebrows. "Now there was me reckoning that you were returning from Wildman's Gulch, a well known spot for outlaws to hole up in, and a spot where Hellfire might have made a base."

"I resent the—" Billy screeched as Alvin slammed a hand on his waist and pulled him down from his horse. Then Alvin stood him straight and facing Lincoln.

"I could have meant I thought you were searching for him. Why did you think I meant you met him?"

Billy gulped. "You can't prove nothing."

"A box back in Stark Pass proves somebody saw Hellfire. You'd better hope nobody suggests to Marshal Cooper that it was you."

"Then I've got no problem," Billy said, not meeting Lincoln's eye. "It wasn't me."

"Except you do know where Hellfire is hiding out." Lincoln advanced a long pace on Billy with his fist raised. "And you will tell me."

"I'll tell you nothing," Billy grunted, firming his jaw.

"My methods aren't as brutal as Hellfire's are, but I reckon I can make you talk." Lincoln slapped his fist into his palm with a resounding crack. "I'd save yourself some pain and just talk."

* * *

"I've got a box for you," Harvey shouted as he scampered up the slope and away from the post.

The caped figure was still 200 yards ahead of him. He had taken fifteen minutes to wriggle out of the ropes that had encased his legs and, as yet, he hadn't found a way to remove the ropes from his hands.

In that time the figure had slipped back from the outcrop. It was now moving away along the top of the ridge, skirting away from the post, its slow speed just keeping it ahead of him and taunting Harvey.

He waved the box above his head and

shouted again, but the caped figure carried on. Harvey put on a burst of speed, making a sharp pain rip through his chest. He staggered to a halt.

With his head lolling, he coughed, freeing his lungs of the cloying tang of smoke. When he'd regained his breath, the figure was cresting the summit of the ridge and disappearing from view.

Without much hope, he shuffled after it, his pace gradually building into a shambling run. It was another ten minutes before he crested the ridge. The terrain ahead was barren and the figure wasn't visible.

He stood with his hands to his brow. The afternoon heat haze made everything shimmer as he searched the barren wilderness for movement, but not even a bird moved. Despite the heat of the sun beating down on his head and his narrow escape from the fire, he shivered.

"Who are you?" he shouted. "Where are you going? What do you want?"

His voice was lost in the vastness. So, with

a shake of the head, he walked back down the side of the ridge, aiming to return to the post. Then marks in the dirt caught his eye. He shuffled closer and discovered that the marks were footprints.

He hunkered down beside them, even fingering them to prove they were real. Then he rolled back on to his haunches and nodded to himself.

"I don't know who you are, where you've gone, or what you want," he said to himself. "But I do know you're not a ghost."

NINE

"There's not as many in the camp as I expected," Alvin said, when he dropped back down behind the boulder.

"Yeah," Daniel said. "I thought Hellfire would have at least a dozen men, but I saw only two."

"It doesn't surprise me," Lincoln said. He sneered at Billy. "I know Hellfire. I reckon this no-good varmint overheard my challenge and told him about it, and Hellfire couldn't resist taking it up. He's gone to Calamity to meet me and left just enough men here to guard Cooper's family."

"Let's hope you're right."

Lincoln snorted his assurance and then settled down. For the next ten minutes they watched the encampment. Hellfire had holed up in Wildman's Gulch, a rocky gash in the wilderness fifteen miles north of Stark

Pass.

He had secured an area at the top of a slope before a sheer crag that provided a wide view of the surrounding area. Behind the camp, under an overhang, there was a cave and, as Hellfire's men had piled wood in the entrance, presumably as a wind-break, Lincoln reckoned it was a reasonable deduction that the hostages were there.

One man was sitting by the dying remnants of a fire. Another man was patrolling back and forth with the bored indifference of someone who didn't expect anyone to approach.

A third man came out of the cave to speak to them and then wandered back inside. Lincoln noted that this man was the most problematic. With a secure location such as the cave to hide in, he could hold them off and, if capture were imminent, take deadly revenge on Cooper's family.

So Lincoln whispered orders to Alvin and Daniel and then backed down the slope. Bent double, he took a circuitous route around the crag that came out on the overhang. He discovered that he was ten yards above and fifty yards to the left of the cave.

He shuffled back from the edge. Aware now of his bearings he headed to a spot above the cave, but as he shuffled to the edge again voices sounded below. He hunkered down and when the voices came again, he realized that they were emerging through a fissure.

The gap was thin and sheer, about three feet wide and set thirty feet from the edge. He shuffled down beside the fissure. The bottom was about forty feet below and it turned toward the edge and then disappeared from his view, but he guessed that it tunneled to the cave.

One of the voices was a woman's and the other was a man's, but he couldn't make out the words. He thought about slipping down the fissure and attacking Hellfire's men from an unexpected direction, but he decided that the fissure was too difficult to traverse quietly.

He shuffled to the edge of the overhang. Below, the men were in the same positions as before. From his elevated position Daniel was visible, but not Alvin, who by now should have reached an outcrop, twenty yards to the right of the cave, but his deputy was well-hidden.

For the next fifteen minutes, he bided his time as he waited until one of the outlaws passed by Alvin's position and Alvin could get a drop on him. His plan was that when that man didn't return, the other outlaw would go to investigate; then Lincoln would mount his rescue attempt.

So, when the patrolling outlaw headed to the outcrop, Lincoln shuffled to the edge, his gun drawn and ready to fire down at the camp. The man shuffled behind the outcrop to be out of the view of the man by the fire.

His hands went to his belt as he moved to squat, but then Alvin leaped out and grabbed him in a neck-hold from behind, his other hand slapping over his mouth. The two men struggled until the outlaw wriggled out from Alvin's grip, forcing Alvin to clip his jaw.

The outlaw staggered back for a pace and then righted himself. He returned a blow that slammed Alvin into the outcrop. His head cracked into the rock and, as he slumped to the ground, the outlaw shouted a warning.

The man by the fire jumped up and broke into a run, ready to repel the ambush. Within seconds he'd be out of Lincoln's sight-line, so Lincoln jumped from the overhang. He crashed on to the man's back, tumbling him to the ground.

Then he grabbed the back of his head and hammered his forehead into the stony ground, knocking him cold. The other outlaw was now running back to confront him; farther away Daniel was running up the slope toward the cave while laying down covering fire.

Lincoln added to the gunfire, but when the approaching outlaw dove for cover behind a boulder Lincoln accepted his exposed position and ran for the cave. He reached it ten paces ahead of Daniel and vaulted the wooden wind barrier in the entrance.

Running toward him from deeper within the cave was the other man and he fired on the run. Lincoln leaped to the side, saving him from a bullet that whined past his head and flew through the cave entrance.

From behind him Daniel fired into the cave, the lead whistling past the running man to zing back and forth across the cave. Lying on his side, Lincoln fired again. His finger twitched on an empty chamber.

In desperation, he rolled to his feet and launched himself at the man. He grabbed his arm and pushed it high. The man wasted a shot into the cave roof, the shot ricocheting around them, and then the two men slammed together.

Outside the cave gunfire ripped out. Lincoln gritted his teeth and ignored it. He pulled back his fist and slugged the man's jaw, but his opponent shrugged off the blow and stamped on Lincoln's foot.

In an involuntary action, Lincoln staggered back, his grip on the outlaw's arm loosening, and the man bundled Lincoln away. Lincoln threw out a hand toward the cave wall to stop himself falling, but his foot slipped in the loose dirt.

He went to his knees, as the outlaw swung his gun down at him and steadied his aim. Then Daniel vaulted the wooden barrier and he tore a slug into the man's left hip. The man staggered to the side as he fired, Daniel's shot veering his aim.

Lead whistled over Lincoln's left shoulder and cannoned into the cave wall. As the man thrust out his right leg and stopped himself falling, Lincoln rose to his feet and charged him.

On the run, he hurled an uppercut to the man's chin that knocked his feet from under him and slammed him into the cave wall before he slid to the ground. The man shook himself. With his hands shaking he aimed his gun at Lincoln, but Daniel took careful aim and thundered repeated gunfire into his chest, his body twitching with each blast before it lay still.

Lincoln nodded his thanks as he reloaded, but his deputy gestured down. Lincoln winced and threw himself to the ground, the action saving him from a burst of gunfire that scythed over his head as it blasted in through the cave entrance.

He rolled over and came up on his belly, his gun thrust out, and fired wildly through the cave entrance. One shot ripped through the chest of the man running toward the cave. Lincoln didn't wait to celebrate his victory and moved to the wind barrier.

Down the slope, the remaining guard had come to and now he and Alvin were locked in a furious battle, both men rolling over each other as each tried to turn his gun on the other. With a barked order to Daniel to cover him Lincoln vaulted the wind barrier and ran down the slope.

He got to within five paces of the fighting twosome when Alvin's opponent slugged Alvin away. Before he could turn his gun on

Alvin, Lincoln hammered a shot into the man's stomach that staggered him back a pace.

The man righted himself and returned fire, his shot pluming into the dirt at Lincoln's feet. So this time, Lincoln nipped a shot into his neck that spun his feet from the ground before he slammed to the earth.

Then he joined Alvin and the lawmen stood poised, waiting for more trouble, but the slope returned to quiet. Lincoln patted Alvin's shoulder and pointed down the slope at Billy, who had taken advantage of the fighting to scurry away.

Lincoln directed Alvin to chase him down and then headed back up the slope, gathering a torch from the dying campfire on the way. Then he paced over the wind barrier and inside. The flames danced shadows across the entrance, but it showed that the cave was deeper than he had first thought with the main bulk of the cave emerging to the side.

Still, he had to duck to avoid scraping his

head on the roof. With the brand held aloft and his heart hammering against what he feared he'd find, he walked deeper into the cave. At the bend, he slowed as two people were whispering to each other – a man and a woman.

Lincoln slipped around the corner. Beyond was a wider recess, twenty yards across, which had sufficient height for Lincoln to stand upright. In the center of the recess Leah huddled beside a child. By the back wall stood a cage and in it was the manacled and hunched form of Shelton Baez.

"Is that you, Lincoln?" he asked, his narrowed eyes flickering with hope.

"It sure is," Lincoln said. He turned to Leah, but she wrapped protecting arms around her child and backed away to the cave wall.

"Stay away from us," she said.

"Don't worry," Shelton said. "He's a U.S. Marshal, and one of the best."

Leah nodded. "Then I sure am glad you're here, but is Jim all right after what Hellfire did to. . . ?"

Leah lowered her head to sob, tears streaming down her cheeks.

"Marshal Cooper was mighty upset by what happened, but he was coping when we left Stark Pass."

"Then we're both grateful."

Lincoln nodded and then gestured for Daniel to tend to her. He hurried across the cave to examine the cage. He tapped the bars, finding them solid, and fingered the lock.

"Where did Hellfire get this?" he asked Shelton.

"It's a cage from the railroad, perhaps for transporting—"

"Money, once," Lincoln said. "I guess he thought the idea amusing."

"Did you go to. . . ?" Shelton gulped when Lincoln nodded.

"Your post was burned to the ground. I guess you've lost everything."

Shelton sighed. "Yeah, I've lost everything."

Lincoln stood back from the cage and drew his gun. He sighted the lock from various angles, but as he considered where the ricochet might land, Alvin dragged the hunched form of Billy into the cave. Shelton's eyes flared as he struggled within his manacles.

"What's that man doing here?" he snarled.

"He was helping us to find you."

"He works for Hellfire," Shelton said, lowering his voice. "I wouldn't trust nothing that man says."

"Hey, I heard that," Billy shouted. "I wouldn't trust anything that snake says either."

Shelton shook his fists, rattling his manacles against the side of the cage, while Billy shouted an oath at him.

"Alvin, Daniel, get Billy and the hostages outside while I free Shelton," Lincoln said.

Daniel helped Leah to her feet, the child throwing her arms around her neck and, with Alvin escorting the grumbling Billy, they headed to the cave entrance. When they'd headed around the corner, Lincoln aimed at the lock and fired. The first three shots cannoned away, but the fourth sprang the lock, letting the door fly open.

Shelton nodded his thanks. "I hope you can do that with these manacles."

"I will, provided you don't move while I'm firing."

As Lincoln sighted the first manacle Alvin shouted a warning from the cave entrance. Then his deputy sprinted around the corner while crying out that Hellfire had returned.

"I said you shouldn't have trusted Billy," Shelton said. "He's led you into a trap."

Lincoln gritted his teeth on hearing this possible truth. He ran past Billy to the cave entrance. As Alvin had reported, down the slope, Hellfire's men had returned. At least fifteen men were taking up secure positions surrounding the cave and just out of firing range.

As Lincoln kneeled down behind the wooden barrier, one of Hellfire's men broke off from the group and ran up the slope.

Lincoln and Alvin fired at him, but the man leaped into a hollow and stayed down.

Presently, a thin stream of smoke plumed up from his position. Then the man himself rose up. He held a burning brand aloft and with an overhand throw he hurled the brand at the cave.

Lincoln ducked, but the brand landed on the wooden barrier which, within seconds, roared into flame. He risked leaning over to try to bat the brand away, but sustained gunfire from below forced him to dive for cover.

By then it was too late and the barrier was alight, the flames roaring up as the wind that funneled into the cave fed the fire. Less than thirty seconds after the brand had landed the flames had spread across the cave entrance, cutting off their escape route.

Lincoln winced, realizing now that the barrier wasn't there to stop the wind. This *was* a trap and Hellfire had stacked the wood in the cave entrance to smoke them out.

TEN

With an arm thrown across his face, Lincoln braved an approach to the cave entrance, but the blistering heat forced him to hurry back.

"Hellfire, you don't want to end it this way," he shouted. "This is just about us. Put out the fire and you can have me, but let the others go."

He lowered his arm as, behind the shimmering wall of flame, Hellfire strode up the slope.

"I heard promises like that sixteen years ago," Hellfire said. "They weren't true then and they aren't true now. You'll die, just like my woman died."

Lincoln opened his mouth to shout at

Hellfire, but then slapped his fist against his thigh, deciding that talking was using up the limited time he had left to find a way to escape. He ran back into the main recess where smoke had already filled the top half of the cave, the swirling barrier lowering.

Alvin was holding Billy by the side wall. Lincoln hurried toward him, grabbed his collar and pulled him up straight.

"What kind of crazy plan was this? You've got us all trapped."

Billy coughed. "I never expected him to do this. You have to believe me."

Lincoln held on to Billy and then snorted. "I guess even you aren't stupid enough to help Hellfire kill you."

He threw Billy to the ground and then gathered his deputies around him.

"What. . . ?" Alvin said and then paused to bark out a racking cough. "What are we going to do?"

Lincoln extracted a kerchief from his pocket and waved it.

"First, put kerchiefs over your mouths to

reduce the smoke. Then, there's a fissure on the top of the overhang. It leads down into this cave. Find it!"

While Alvin and Daniel headed off to explore the extremities of the cave, Billy slumped down by the wall. As he'd found a location that was a safe distance from the flames in the entrance, Lincoln ordered Leah and Mollie to lie on the ground beside him.

Then he ran to the cage. He climbed inside and fingered the manacles, finding that the bands that secured Shelton's wrist had a lock, but a chain connected them to the cage. Lincoln directed Shelton to duck and then shot through the chains.

The freed Shelton grunted his approval while slapping Lincoln's back. When they'd slipped out of the cage Alvin and Daniel were already pointing at the smoke that was curling toward the back of the cave, suggesting that the fissure was there, drawing the smoke in that direction.

The smoke had already filled the cave

down to head level. Even with the kerchief over his mouth Lincoln had to fight down the urge to cough with every breath. With the urgency for escaping growing with every passing second, the group needed no encouragement to trail from the cave and down the short tunnel at the back.

In the growing darkness they squeezed over a clutter of boulders and down an incline. Then the light-level grew until they stood below the fissure. It was a vertical chimney, about forty feet high, but with handholds and several ledges.

Lincoln directed Daniel to help Leah climb and Alvin to carry the child. Leah objected, but a shake of the head from Lincoln encouraged her to relent. Behind him, Shelton screeched.

Lincoln turned, finding that Billy had jumped him and the two men were struggling on the ground. Each man had his hands planted on the other's neck and was trying to squeeze and wrestle the other man on to his back.

Lincoln ordered Alvin and Leah to begin the ascent. Then he slapped a hand on Billy's shoulder and pulled him away, but that only gave Shelton enough room to firm his footing and launch another attack on Billy. So Lincoln grabbed Shelton's collar and pulled him back.

"We've got just a few minutes to get out of here," he said with the two men held at arm's length. "Whatever this is about can wait."

Billy launched a fist at Shelton, but it fell short and Shelton directed a kick at Billy, which also fell short. Even when Lincoln shook them the men continued to struggle. Then the smoke funneling out through the fissure dragged a pained burst of coughing from both of them.

They nodded reluctantly and backed away from each other. Lincoln snorted his disgust for them and then directed Shelton to climb the fissure after Daniel. He held Billy back and only let him climb when Shelton was ten feet above his head.

Then Lincoln started climbing. The fissure was thin, but this enabled Lincoln to plant a hand on either side and, with his back braced, head upward. One by the one they emerged on to the ground above and rolled away from the smoke pouring out of the fissure.

Lincoln clambered out last. Like the others, he dragged away his kerchief and lay on his back, while drawing in long breaths. Around him the others were coughing so Lincoln rolled to his knees.

"We all want to get the smoke out of our lungs, but do it quietly," he said. "Hellfire might hear us."

He was answered with several nods and a few suppressed coughs. Then, on his belly, he shuffled to the edge of the overhang. The smoke pluming from the wooden barrier obscured his vision, but below him were the shimmering outlines of Hellfire and his men, who were milling before the cave entrance.

He debated ambushing them, but as his

deputies were still lying on their backs with their chests heaving, he accepted they were in no shape to mount an effective assault. Though their horses were only fifty yards away from the cave Lincoln reckoned they probably couldn't get to them.

From the intensity of the heat rippling up from the cave entrance, Lincoln judged that the fire would burn for another hour. That gave them enough time to get some distance away from Hellfire.

Even then, Stark Pass was fifteen miles away; Calamity was ten miles distant. He turned, but at that moment, Billy was dragging himself to his feet. Then he launched himself at Shelton.

Lincoln winced and gestured at them to stop fighting, but both men ignored him and Alvin had his back to him as he helped Leah and Mollie to crawl away from the fissure. Daniel was on his back, gasping.

Lincoln rolled to his feet and, keeping his head down, ran toward them. Both men were now slugging it out with round-armed blows and much kicking of dirt. Such a commotion had to attract Hellfire's attention before long.

Then Billy dragged himself free of Shelton's clutches and delivered a punch that knocked his opponent toward the opening of the fissure. Shelton teetered on the edge, his arms wheeling as he fought for balance.

Billy rolled his shoulders and charged him, aiming to push him over the edge, but at the last second, Shelton half-slipped, half-hurled himself to the side to land on his belly with his feet dangling over the edge. Billy jabbed in a heel, trying to halt his progress, but he skidded past Shelton and tumbled into the hole.

With an echoing shriek, he clattered down it, his shrieking dying as he crashed to the bottom. A puff of smoke billowed up as Shelton slipped another foot down the hole. He tore his fingers into the dirt as he searched for purchase, but he continued to slip.

Inch by inexorable inch he slid away, so

Lincoln ran at full tilt: he threw himself to the ground and skidded on his belly to grab Shelton's clawed hand as it slipped from view. They locked hands, Shelton's body dangling above the smoky void.

Billy was lying at the bottom, his neck presenting a sharp angle. Then the smoke rolled over him and Shelton's weight and the lack of purchase on the ground dragged Lincoln toward the edge.

Lincoln planted his elbows wide, but Shelton's weight still dragged him over the ground. He scrambled his legs, but that only sped his movement. Then arms wrapped around his chest and stopped him. He was just nodding his thanks to Daniel when he realized the hands were Leah's.

"Be careful," he urged. "I'm heavier than you are."

"Then don't struggle," she said. "Daniel's coming. I'll hold you until then."

Lincoln nodded. Within moments another pair of hands landed on his back and dragged him and Shelton out and on to solid ground. They lay for a moment, gasping. Then Lincoln directed them to get away from the hole and draw breath behind a heap of boulders that lay fifty yards from the fissure, a safe distance from the edge of the overhang.

Everyone nodded their approval and scurried to safety. Lincoln expected that the combination of the smoke filtering out through the fissure and Billy's shriek would alert Hellfire, but after ten minutes Hellfire still hadn't come to investigate and Lincoln started to plan their next action.

"What's wrong?" Shelton asked when Lincoln shuffled to his side.

"I'm just wondering if I can trust you," Lincoln said.

"Did I need a good reason to fight that snake?"

"I guess not, but once I get us out of this, I'll want to know what you were fighting about."

Shelton sighed. "Does that mean you don't know already?"

Lincoln frowned. "I reckon that sixteen years ago Billy was either a poor lawman or he was trying to help Hellfire get away. If you've got something else to tell me, it'd be better for you if you just volunteered it."

Shelton lowered his head, suggesting he was wondering how much Lincoln already knew.

"I guess I've wanted to tell someone about this for years." Shelton took a deep breath. "Amid all the shooting and confusion, I escaped and found the fifty thousand dollars. I figured Billy was planning to steal it and would come back for it later, so I hid it, figuring that when I found someone I could trust, I'd give it to them. What with having to make a fresh start after the fire, I got to thinking. . . ."

"What about Billy?"

"He always reckoned I'd found it, but he couldn't prove nothing."

Lincoln nodded. "I can't say how bad that is for you."

Shelton looked skyward, his eyes

watering. "It's already worse than you can imagine. That secret cost me everything."

ELEVEN

"I'm here," Harvey shouted, his voice echoing back to him from the abandoned buildings along Calamity's main drag. "I've come here to see you."

He waited – not that he expected an immediate answer. He had tried to find the woman's footprints, but had found no more signs of her passage. When she'd disappeared she had been heading toward Calamity, and Harvey couldn't believe she would go anywhere else but here, or that Shelton hadn't meant him to do anything other than find this woman when he had directed him to give 'her' this box.

After he had freed the ropes from his hands he had tried to prize open the box, but a clasp held the lid firm. A keyhole confirmed that he'd have to find the key or break it open to get inside.

"I'm here," he shouted again.

There wasn't much to the town, just two rows of standing buildings, so it took Harvey only five minutes to roam the length of the main drag. Then he explored the buildings. Dirt and dust had accumulated in their shells.

In each he found no sign that anyone had been through here, and certainly no sign that anyone lived here. Sightings of a ghost in Calamity had been common and had helped to keep people away, but if someone had been living here, and perhaps fueling those ghost rumors, they needed a base.

None of the buildings were likely places for anyone to live in. Only when he reached the station did he find recent horse-prints. As far as he could tell the riders had just stopped beside the station and then moved on. He didn't think they had anything to do with the woman.

"I'm Harvey Baez," he shouted, but his voice wasn't much louder than the wind that swirled and whined between the buildings. "Shelton sent me. Something terrible has happened to him. Hellfire kidnapped him and I want to save him. I think you can help me."

Harvey stood on the platform, hoping that whatever bond Shelton felt for this woman was mutual, but when he didn't get an answer, he paraded around on the spot, waving the box above his head.

"Shelton told me to find you and give you this. I have no idea what it is or what it means, but it's important that you get it."

Harvey kneeled and placed the box on the edge of the platform. Fired by his desire to resolve the mystery of who she was and what she wanted, he investigated the town again while ignoring the station.

This time his thorough investigation discovered many places where someone could hide: under the boardwalk, beneath the saloon, amid the ruined remnants of the disintegrating stable. Aside from rodents nobody had lived in any of these places. When he returned to the station the box was still where he'd left it.

"I know you're hiding here somewhere," Harvey shouted, picking up the box and holding it aloft. "I'm not leaving until you see me. I just hope you don't wait long. Because I reckon you're the only person who can save Shelton's life."

Harvey walked back down the main drag. He didn't expect a quick answer, but to his surprise someone hollered behind him. He turned around, but the town was deserted. Then he realized that the holler had come from out of town.

Riders were heading down the side of the railroad tracks. After all the bad luck of the last few hours Harvey had no doubt that Hellfire was among those men.

* * *

Lincoln sought his deputies' views as to

their next action. Alvin thought Calamity was a good place to hole up. Daniel reckoned they should go to Stark Pass, as they could ensure Leah and Mollie's safety there.

Lincoln decided to take the best parts of both plans. He directed Daniel to head to Stark Pass and fetch help, while he led the rest on a direct route to Calamity. Then they walked for an hour with Alvin trailing behind and swiping away the obvious signs of their trail.

They covered several miles, by which time Lincoln judged that Hellfire would have been able to get into the cave and discover that they had escaped. It was only a matter of time before he came after them.

Sure enough, when the weary group reached the edge of an incline, two miles from Calamity, from where they overlooked the railroad tracks, a troop of men rode into view. These men didn't include Hellfire, but they were searching for them.

From the way they repeatedly examined the ground, Lincoln reckoned they had picked up a trail, but had now lost it. One of the riders stopped and drew the others around him. They milled.

Then the lead man gesticulated and two men hurried along the tracks while another two peeled off and headed up the slope. Lincoln slipped back from the edge and joined Alvin while Shelton, Leah and Mollie sat beside a boulder.

"They picked up a trail, but it isn't ours," Alvin said.

"You'll get no argument there," Lincoln said. "That won't matter if they accidentally find us."

Alvin nodded, and after a short debate they agreed upon the route that the men would take when they reached the top of the slope. As that route headed between two large sentinel rocks, Lincoln and Alvin hurried there and climbed up either side of the rocks to their tops.

Lincoln lay flat on his front. When hoofs clopped as the men approached them, he exchanged gestures with Alvin on the other rock and then shuffled to the edge. Lincoln stood up, still keeping back to stay out of sight.

Then, on the count of three, he and Alvin leaped from the rocks. Lincoln slammed onto the right-hand rider's shoulders, knocking him from his horse. He was aware of Alvin also unseating his target.

Then the two men hit the ground and rolled over, their limbs entangled. Lincoln's opponent struggled out from under him, but Lincoln's right cross to the chin knocked him back on his haunches and his second blow to the cheek pole-axed him.

Alvin had fallen awkwardly and his opponent had rolled clear. That man gained his footing first and, as Lincoln turned to them, he slugged Alvin's jaw, crashing him on to his back. Lincoln ran to him, aiming to silently subdue him, but when the man drew his gun and aimed it down at the sprawling Alvin, Lincoln had no choice but to blast lead into his back, sending him sprawling.

As the gunfire echoes faded to silence

Lincoln confirmed that the man was dead; he dragged Alvin to his feet and ordered him to secure the horses. Then he ran to the edge of the slope, hanging on to the hope that the group below wouldn't interpret the gunfire as anything more than their colleagues' exuberance.

Below, the group exchanged a set of barked orders. Then they trooped toward the slope and hurried up it. Lincoln assured himself that they were intent on attacking them. Then he rolled back from the edge, and to his irritation Alvin and Shelton had rounded up only one of the horses.

The other horse was galloping away and heading toward the edge of the slope, throwing up its heels in a way that suggested they wouldn't capture it in the short time they had before the men found them. As Shelton joined him Lincoln searched for the best place to make their stand.

"We can still make it to Calamity and make a stand there," Shelton said.

"We could, but we've only got one horse

and it isn't carrying all of us," Lincoln said.

Shelton stood tall and patted the gun he'd taken off the unconscious outlaw.

"It will if I stay behind. Just get the child and the woman to safety and forget about me."

Lincoln didn't waste a second thinking about the offer.

"Shelton, I wouldn't be a lawman if I did that."

"Then just go anyhow. I stole and I'll pay the price for that later, but I'd sooner pay for it here, getting revenge on the men who killed . . . on these men."

When Shelton gave an encouraging nod Lincoln patted his back and turned away before he could persuade himself this was a bad idea. He mounted the horse. Alvin slipped in behind him and reached down to help Leah and the child up to sit on his lap. With so much weight, the horse wouldn't be able to carry them far, but Calamity was less than two miles away.

"What's Shelton doing?" Alvin asked.

"He isn't coming," Lincoln said as he headed to the top of the slope.

As Alvin murmured in understanding the riders swung around to head through the sentinel rocks. So, picking their route gingerly, they arced down the slope toward the tracks. As the rocks disappeared from view, Shelton had already taken cover.

Still, Lincoln gave a silent salute and concentrated on finding a safe route down to the railroad tracks. Then behind them gunfire ripped out, the sounds echoing back and forth between the high rocks.

It was sustained and ferocious, the blasts seemingly reporting from many directions as Shelton gave the men a battle. Lincoln firmed his jaw and hurried on. When they reached ground level and the side of the tracks, the gunfire spluttered to silence.

Lincoln winced and encouraged the horse to attain the fastest speed it could. At a fair trot, they headed down the side of the tracks toward Calamity. He dreaded the moment when the men worked out where they had gone and headed after them, but they got closer to Calamity with still no sign of pursuit.

The sun was edging toward the horizon, casting a long shadow before them as they swung around to head down the main drag, but then a plume of dust rose up beyond the railroad tracks. Within seconds it resolved into the forms of the pursuing riders.

Lincoln slowed to search for the best place to mount their defense when Hellfire's men did arrive. They trotted past the station and Lincoln drew his horse to a halt beside the saloon, the hard-pressed steed rearing.

The pursuers *were* closing on them, now just a mile back, but that wasn't the worst of their problems. There, in the center of town, was the very cage in which Hellfire had previously imprisoned Shelton.

"Why is that here?" Alvin said.

"Because Hellfire's already here," Lincoln said.

TWELVE

From all around, gunfire exploded – from the ruined wreckage of the stable, from the store, from both ends of the town. Lincoln yanked the reins to the side, aiming to gallop out of town, but a slug thudded into the horse's flank and forced it to stumble.

With no choice, Lincoln jumped from the saddle. Along with Alvin, they stood on either side of Leah and Mollie. The shooting was relentless, the slugs whining all around them. So they ran to the only place from where gunfire wasn't coming, the saloon.

As they clattered on to the boardwalk, two men bobbed up to fire at them through the broken windows. Lincoln and Alvin had already committed themselves to seeking cover here, so Lincoln charged through the doorway, kicking open the only batwing, while Alvin leaped through the right-hand window.

Lincoln jumped to the side and blasted the man by the left-hand window, making him stumble and fall through the window to land on the boardwalk outside. On the run, Alvin tore gunfire into the second man, spinning him around to slam into the wall and slide to the floor.

Then they covered Leah and the child as they hurried in after them. Lincoln positioned Leah and Mollie behind the remnants of the bar and then hunkered down beside the door. Gunfire still peppered the saloon wall sporadically, but from it Lincoln judged the number of men they were facing.

By his estimate at least a dozen men had taken over Calamity. Groups had stationed themselves at the edge of town in both directions and others fired around the sides of the stable and the store. In the shell of the building opposite another group of men had congregated, but as yet he hadn't located Hellfire.

"Hellfire, attacking a U.S. Marshal is a big mistake," he shouted.

"I have nothing to say to you, Lincoln Hawk," Hellfire shouted from the town store.

"Neither are you getting any closer to that fifty thousand dollars."

"I reckon I am. Somebody knows where it is and I reckon you're that somebody."

Lincoln searched for another taunt, but then decided to remain quiet. He'd done the more important thing and located him.

"Alvin, secure the back," he said. "Leah, you stay where you are. Mollie, you go to sleep."

Presently, three riders emerged from the gathering gloom to gallop into town. Lincoln relayed this information to Alvin, not mentioning that these were the men who had overcome Shelton, although, as their numbers had reduced considerably, Shelton had clearly given better than he'd received.

These men dismounted fifty yards from the saloon as Hellfire's men used the distraction to edge closer, but Lincoln sprayed wild gunfire at them and forced them to dive for cover.

"If that's the best they can do, we will prevail," Lincoln said, hurrying the last man into cover with a final gunshot.

"Yeah, these men aren't that impressive," Alvin said with a wink from his position at the back door.

Lincoln settled down beside the window, unable to suppress a smile as he prepared for a short siege. Daniel had headed to Stark Pass and although that town was five miles farther away than Calamity, his deputy had been traveling alone and so should have been able to reach there by now.

That meant a posse should be coming here to rescue them before long. Lincoln only had to hold out until then. To ensure Hellfire's men didn't feel confident and storm the saloon, Lincoln provided sporadic gunfire that peppered the surrounding buildings, but as none of the men showed themselves he didn't hit anyone.

That didn't concern Lincoln. Every minute that he kept them at bay was another minute less that they had to wait for the posse. Time passed slowly as the cage outside caught the sun's last rays and darkness descended, but the moon was nearly full and provided sufficient light to give Lincoln a decent view of the scene.

At the back door Alvin kept lookout and Leah murmured a low and soothing lullaby to her daughter. Just as Lincoln detected a growing level of confidence in himself that they could last out, scrambling sounded, as of someone clambering over the roof.

The roof covered only half of the saloon, and the part that was covered didn't look strong enough to support a bird, never mind a man. When the scrambling noise sounded again, Alvin cocked his head to the side, trying to identify from where the sound was coming, but it was Leah who raised a hand to attract Lincoln's attention and then she pointed downward.

Lincoln nodded, realizing that she was right and that somebody was crawling about *under* the saloon. Everyone turned to a hole in the floor behind the bar. Then Leah screamed and rocked back as a man climbed out of that hole.

"Reach," Lincoln said, sighting the man down the barrel of his gun.

"Don't shoot," the man screeched and hurled his hands aloft.

His whole body shook with suppressed fear causing Lincoln to flinch back when he realized that the man was only a boy, perhaps aged fourteen or fifteen. He held a box aloft in a raised hand and his eyes were wide and scared.

"Now, son, are you sure you're old enough to be one of Hellfire's hired guns?"

"I'm no hired gun, sir. I'm Harvey Baez. I was hiding when I heard you talking and my uncle always said I should trust Marshal Lincoln Hawk."

"Your uncle is a wise man. Is he. . . ?"

"He's Shelton Baez," Harvey said.

Lincoln gritted his teeth to suppress a wince. "I understand. Now lower your hands and join Leah. You're in no danger while you're with me."

Harvey gave a nervous nod and then dropped his hands to his side.

"I trust you, but you have to get that Hellfire," he said as he joined Leah. "He took my uncle and I reckon he might have killed him."

"Perhaps when this over we can find out what happened to him," Lincoln said, as Alvin winced and Leah lowered her head.

To avoid the uncomfortable subject, Lincoln hunkered down beside the door and fired two quick shots at the store opposite, but his enticing firing couldn't persuade Hellfire to return fire. With only limited ammunition, Lincoln desisted.

Within the saloon everyone remained calm. Lincoln was pleased that despite the occasional scare Leah continued to sing to

Mollie, but Harvey was watching the man Alvin had shot when they'd first come into the saloon. Then he shuffled across the saloon and collected the man's gun.

"Are you sure you're safe with that gun, son?" Lincoln asked.

Harvey headed back across the saloon and sat against the bar with the gun cradled in his lap.

"I reckon I can aim and fire." He leaned back to place the box on the bar and hefted the weapon. "I might not hit anything, but it might help."

Harvey's hand shook and, to try to take his mind off the fear the young man was clearly feeling, Lincoln pointed at the box on the bar.

"What's in the box?"

Harvey flinched, as if he were realizing for the first time that he'd brought the box with him.

"My uncle gave it to me just before Hellfire took him. I have to give it to someone."

"Who is that *someone*?"

Harvey's eyes glazed. "I don't know for sure. I've got an idea who he meant, but she can't be . . . I don't know for sure, just that I had to give it to her, but he never said who *her* was."

"And you don't know what's in the box?"

"I don't, sir. It's locked and I don't have the key."

Lincoln raised his eyebrows. "Do you mind if I open it for you?"

Harvey took the box from the bar and slid it across the saloon floor. It stopped four feet short of Lincoln, but, with one eye closed, Lincoln sighted the box and blasted the clasp away.

The force tumbled the box end over end, but when it came to a halt, the lid had opened. Lincoln checked that nobody from outside could see him move and then crawled to the box. He picked it up and returned to the window.

Aside from a folded slip of paper the box was empty. With his brow furrowed Lincoln removed the paper and read it, and then snorted.

"One bag of corn, a side of salted beef," he read.

"It's a list of provisions," Harvey said.

"Yeah." Lincoln pointed at Harvey. "Is this some kind of joke?"

"No, this is what Shelton gave me to give to her."

"The list, or the provisions?" Alvin said.

"What are you thinking?" Lincoln asked, turning to his deputy.

"Shelton was a trading man. Perhaps he didn't want to disappoint a customer."

Alvin murmured a laugh, but Lincoln just snarled, silencing his good humor, and then shook his head.

"There's something I'm not seeing here."

Lincoln read the list again, but however he looked at it, the list was just a list of food and enough to keep one person fed for at least a month. He held the list up to the window, but there was no more writing on it.

He fingered the box, but there was nothing else to it. If Shelton had stolen the $50,000, a last note like this ought to provide a clue as to its location, but Lincoln couldn't see that this helped. He placed the note back in the box and kicked it across the floor to Harvey, who read the note and sighed.

"This must be wrong," he said.

Lincoln assumed that Harvey's shaking hands meant he had expected something else, but as he considered how he could push him for more details without worrying him, Alvin raised a hand.

"Lincoln, you'd better come and see this," he said from the back door. "They're moving into position and I reckon this time they're planning to take us."

Lincoln joined Alvin at the back door and a man was scurrying through the gloom to hide in a hollow. Then, at the front, several men hurried to new positions. He had a deputy, a scared woman and child, and a frightened young man, who, from the loose way he held his gun, was in greater danger of shooting off his own foot than killing any of Hellfire's men.

Hellfire had at least a dozen men, and they were only the ones Lincoln had seen. From the steady way they edged forward, each time under covering gunfire, they had a plan to secure the best strategic positions around the saloon.

"Daniel will be here with that posse soon," Lincoln announced. "We just need to hang on for a while longer."

Harvey was cowering at the corner of the bar and Leah had picked up a length of wood, the only weapon she could find. She'd tucked Mollie behind the bar. Then he waited until Hellfire's men were close enough to present tempting targets.

He didn't have to wait long. They hollered orders to each other, more to instill fear than to organize themselves. Then a wave of men charged for the saloon in an all-out assault, every man firing on the run.

Lincoln returned fire, catching one man in

a high shot that wheeled him to the ground and a second man with a low shot that cut his legs from under him. The rest redoubled their firing and, with the last shards of glass from the window cascading around him, Lincoln had to duck.

Lincoln waited for a lull and bobbed up. He was shocked to find the main drag was clear, every man presumably having gained cover nearer to the saloon. Then, at the back exit, Alvin fired frantically through the door.

Lincoln realized that the run was just a ruse to get men around the back of the saloon and launch their assault from there. Gunfire blasted through the back door, forcing Alvin to retreat, but he kept firing outside.

Then a man stepped into the doorway. Alvin hammered a slug into his chest, but a second man vaulted over this man's tumbling body and dove to the floor. Alvin's shot scythed over the man's head.

Lincoln took longer aim and slammed lead into the man's side, whirling him away.

His second shot thudded into his body. With a last, dying finger-twitch, the man blasted a slug into Alvin.

The shot hit him high, blood flying as it tore through his shoulder. Alvin staggered back, and as his free hand rose to clutch his wound, three men charged through the door and peppered a volley of gunfire across the saloon, which forced Lincoln to dive for cover behind a table.

Alvin went down in a hail of gunfire, bullets tearing into his chest as he staggered backward. Lincoln gained cover, but then discovered that he wasn't their target. The group covered one man who ran to the bar and grabbed Leah, batting the plank from her hands before she'd been able to get in a single retaliatory blow.

As a second man scooped up Mollie, Harvey bobbed up at the end of the bar, but then dove for cover. When Lincoln rose up the leading man turned Leah to face him, using her body as a human shield.

Then they backed away to the door and

outside. The moment they'd slipped through the door Lincoln hurried across the room, but then gunfire ripped out at the front of the saloon.

Lincoln wavered for a moment and then fast-crawled to the window. Daniel and Marshal Cooper were galloping into town, with Daniel firing to the left and right. Lincoln breathed a sigh of relief and laid down a burst of covering gunfire that forced Hellfire's men to stay down.

Daniel and Cooper dismounted. Daniel was at the back, but as he covered Cooper two of Hellfire's men dared to leap out from the stable. Lincoln fired at the first man, knocking him to the ground, but the second man dropped to lie on his belly and delivered a slug to the stomach that wheeled Daniel on to the boardwalk.

Lincoln hammered two shots into this man, rolling him on to his back, as Cooper slid to a halt in the saloon doorway. Then he dashed back and, with Lincoln covering him, helped Daniel into the saloon.

"I sure am glad to see you," Lincoln said, taking Daniel's shoulder and helping Cooper drag him inside.

"We almost didn't make it," Daniel said, clutching his guts as Lincoln propped him up against the wall beside the door. "But I said I'd come."

A red flood cascaded over Daniel's clawed hands, but Lincoln smiled and patted his shoulder.

"We'll be fine now you're here."

Daniel nodded and then slumped to lie on his side. A bubble of blood rippled over his lips, his breathing too shallow to remove it. Lincoln turned to Cooper.

"Where's the rest?" he snapped.

"You've just got me," Cooper said. "I'm a lawman and lawmen are best suited to deal with the likes of Hellfire. I don't waste the lives of my townsfolk."

"You have the right to raise a posse."

"Don't tell me what I can do." Cooper frowned. "Now, where's my wife?"

Lincoln sighed. "If you'd gotten here two

minutes earlier, she'd have been safe behind the bar, but Hellfire's men ambushed me and took her."

"And you just let them?"

Lincoln threw his hands wide apart, signifying the ruined saloon and the rest of Calamity.

"Unless you hadn't noticed, I'm heavily outnumbered here."

"You should have thought of that before you tried your ridiculous rescue attempt. Rescuing her was my job."

Lincoln gestured to the outside. "Then I'd be most obliged to hear your idea of how we get her back."

"I've done plenty of thinking." Cooper waited until Lincoln edged his gun through the window and then aimed his gun at Lincoln's side. "I have to hand you over."

"Watch out," Harvey shouted from the side of the bar and raised his gun to aim at Cooper's back.

"Like Harvey implied – lower that gun, Cooper," Lincoln said.

"Take that gun off me, boy," Cooper said. "The way it's shaking, I doubt you could hit me."

"I can try," Harvey said.

"Harvey, don't shoot a lawman," Lincoln said. "Cooper will put down his gun."

Harvey shuffled the gun into his grip, but then, with a sad shake of the head, lowered the weapon and slapped it on to the bar.

"I'm still not putting down my gun," Cooper said. "I promised Hellfire I'd hand you over, and I will."

Lincoln ignored Cooper's gun and sighted the heap of barrels across the main drag.

"I couldn't decide before if you were yellow-bellied or incompetent. I never thought you were corrupt."

"I have no choice. I can't let my family die."

Lincoln drew his gun back through the window, but he held it high and away from Cooper.

"They're dead already – that's the basis you work on. I know Hellfire. He's cruel. He enjoys seeing people suffer, and you're suffering. If you hand me over, he'll still kill you and your family, so you have nothing to lose by doing your duty."

Cooper gestured upward with his gun so Lincoln stood up and took a steady pace toward him.

"I have to take that chance. We're lawmen. We know the risks, but my family doesn't." Cooper stood back and gestured for Lincoln to drop his gun and head to the door. "I'll give you this – once I've handed you over, if I get out this alive I'll turn in my star and take the consequences."

Lincoln let his gun fall from his fingers. He took long and deliberate paces toward the door, but he stopped one pace away.

"What will it be like for them, living with the knowledge of what you did?"

"At least they'll be alive to worry about it."

"There are worse things than death."

"Tell that to my daughter." Cooper pushed Lincoln through the door.

THIRTEEN

"Lincoln Hawk, I've waited for this moment," Hellfire said, walking toward the saloon with his men flanking him.

On the edge of the crumbling boardwalk, Lincoln wheeled to a halt and stood with his legs planted wide apart.

"Cooper, there's still time to do the right thing," he said.

Inside the saloon, Cooper grabbed Harvey's arm and dragged him outside, and then kicked Lincoln forward.

"I've done what you asked, Hellfire," he said. "Now, free my family like you promised."

"I guess you've completed on your side of the bargain."

Hellfire clicked his fingers and Burl dragged Leah out from the alleyway beside the saloon. He pushed her forward. Leah stared in open-mouthed shock at Lincoln, as Cooper ran toward her.

She shook herself and then held her arms out for Cooper and her to embrace. Then Cooper bent and picked up Mollie and the three hugged with their heads bowed. Leah shared eye contact with Lincoln, but Burl broke up the group and pushed Cooper, and then Leah and Mollie toward the saloon.

He collected Harvey. This time they all ignored Lincoln as they trooped inside, leaving Lincoln standing alone before Hellfire.

"Did you enjoy seeing that family reunited?" Hellfire asked as he paraded back and forth in front of Lincoln.

Lincoln folded his arms and stood with one leg slightly bent, feigning a casual attitude as he waited for the right moment to launch an assault on Hellfire.

"Of course I did."

"Then that'll fortify you against what's

coming."

Hellfire chuckled and maintained the chuckle long after any real humor would have died. His false good mood dragged an echoing snort of laughter from his men. Hellfire directed Burl to go behind Lincoln.

Then rough hands took hold of him. Lincoln struggled, but a second set of hands grabbed him and pulled him back. While rubbing his hands with barely suppressed glee, Hellfire ordered two of his largest men to pummel Lincoln.

Neither man needed any encouragement to plow into him. The first man launched a flurry of short blows to Lincoln's stomach, and then round-armed blows to his face that rocked his head one way and then the other.

Lincoln rolled with the punches, limiting their damage and hoping the men would tire themselves out, but if they were capable of tiring, they took their time. Time ceased to have meaning as Lincoln's world contracted to the systematic blows he was receiving.

He ebbed on the edge of consciousness

and might have passed out because he suddenly realized that the blows had stopped and the pressure holding his arms had receded. Taking this as his chance, Lincoln lurched forward, ready to make a run for Hellfire.

The blows had been worse than he feared and instead of the flat-out charge he expected, he staggered two paces and then fell to his knees. Hellfire laughed and kicked out, the toe of his boot connecting with Lincoln's chin and cracking his head back.

Darkness descended on Lincoln, but only for a moment. Hands grabbed his arms and pulled them high. Then they wrapped ropes around his wrists. He struggled, but he had only enough strength to produce an ineffectual wriggle.

Then his arms pulled taut, the muscles creaking with the strain and shocking him to full awareness. He shook his head, freeing the blood from his eyes to see the dirt was only inches from his face.

The dirt moved, his cheek rasping along

the ground. He raised his head, but still he moved. Then he realized what was happening. Hellfire's men had tied him to a horse and Burl was dragging him along.

Luckily, the short main drag was a solid hardpan with few stones, but Burl turned at the station and trotted back. On either side of the main drag, Hellfire's men lined up to cheer Burl on as Lincoln ripped and bounced along the ground between them.

Burl turned and headed past them for a second pass, and then a third. However much Lincoln bunched his arms, he couldn't relieve the continuous strain and the clothes on his back must have worn through because every jar tore his skin.

Then Burl stopped and someone sliced through the rope. Lincoln lay on his back, enjoying the relief for his strained shoulder muscles, but Burl dismounted and began a persistent kicking of Lincoln's ribs that forced him to roll away and stagger to his feet. He tried to stand upright and face Hellfire, but he could only stand stooped, his arms hanging slackly before him.

"Are you ready to talk?" Hellfire asked, as he swaggered up to Lincoln.

Hellfire raised Lincoln's head by the hair. He slapped his face and then delivered a sharp uppercut that crashed Lincoln on his back. As Lincoln floundered Hellfire kicked out, crunching his boot into Lincoln's ribs and sending him rolling. When Lincoln came to a halt, he shuffled around to kneel.

"Is that the best you can do?" he said through his torn lips.

"No, it isn't," Hellfire said, drawing back his boot. "I've only just started on you."

* * *

When Hellfire finally tired of questioning Lincoln, his men dragged him into the cage, locked it and paraded around it. Early in his ordeal Lincoln had gathered that Hellfire didn't want to actually kill him, although he presumed that that was only because he was saving him until he learned whether he knew anything about the location of the missing money.

After which, he'd kill him. So while he waited for an opportunity to retaliate, his only choice was to endure the punishment and hope he still had the strength afterward to do something. On his knees, Lincoln shuffled to the front of the cage.

"Have you had enough?" he said.

"Nope," Hellfire said. "Are you ready to tell me what you know about the fifty thousand dollars?"

"It's long gone."

"If that's the answer, you're looking at death."

"Why? I spared your life sixteen years ago."

"You did, but not my woman's life," Hellfire snapped, his blemish reddening as he snorted his breath through his nostrils.

Slowly, he calmed down, his head cocked to one side as he appeared to await a response. Lincoln didn't give him the satisfaction and ignored him. So Hellfire gestured to Burl, who, along with three other men, headed into the collapsed stable.

They returned with their arms loaded with wood and piled it around the base of the cage. Then they returned to the stable to collect more.

"What are you doing?" Lincoln asked.

"You die at sunup, just like Adele died," Hellfire said.

Hellfire then headed into the saloon. Marshal Cooper was there and with just his eyes, Lincoln implored the lawman to accept that Hellfire would kill everyone after he'd killed him, but Cooper turned away, leaving Burl to pile even more wood around the cage.

* * *

Harvey hunched at the end of the bar and shivered as Hellfire strode into the saloon. If Hellfire recognized him as the person he'd trapped in the burning trading post he gave no hint.

The last few hours had been terrible as he tried and failed to overcome his shame at his lack of action during Hellfire's onslaught. He had been too terrified to act when Hellfire had ambushed the trading post, and gut-wrenching fear had paralyzed him when Marshal Cooper had turned on Lincoln.

Now he was too scared to do anything but sit quietly and hope Hellfire didn't notice him. Worse, he could see no way to redeem himself. Hellfire headed over to Mollie, and the girl cowered back to press herself into Leah's skirts.

"Stay away from her," Leah snapped, placing a hand in front of her child.

"I won't hurt my favorite little girl." Hellfire hunkered down beside Mollie and patted her shoulder. "I just want to keep her amused."

"I'm too tired," Mollie said, knuckling her eyes and flinching away from Hellfire's touch.

"Then wake up," Hellfire snapped, his eyes

blazing. Then he softened his expression. "Won't you?"

She cringed. "I don't want to."

"You're not scared of me, are you?"

Mollie pouted. "A little, I guess."

"There's no reason for that."

"There's every reason," Leah snapped. "You killed her baby sister."

"I didn't!" Hellfire snarled, flinching back. He pointed at the marshal. "I didn't want to harm anyone, but that man double-crossed me."

He rolled back onto his haunches and then stood up and walked to the back exit. He turned and paced back to the door before returning to the exit. At the far extent of one of his passages, Leah shuffled closer to her husband.

"Do you really reckon this man will free us?" she asked.

Cooper shrugged. "I hope so, but whatever happens, I'll do whatever I have to do to get us out of this."

"I don't care about us, just Mollie." Leah

snuffled and lowered her head.

Cooper shuffled closer to her and placed a consoling hand on her back. Farther along the bar, this comment ground into Harvey's thoughts. He wanted to find a way to redeem himself. As Hellfire's footfalls stomped across the saloon's rotted floor, an idea came to him, so he shuffled along the side of the bar to sit beside Leah.

"If you're only bothered about getting Mollie to safety, I have a plan," he whispered from the corner of his mouth.

"Then do it," Leah snapped.

"Leah!" Cooper said, his comment making Burl turn to them.

"I don't care if I die, as long as Mollie lives," she whispered when Burl turned away.

"What kind of life will that be for her?"

Leah frowned as she thought about this comment, but Harvey laid a hand on Leah's arm.

"It'll be a good one," he said. "Both my parents died when I was young, but Shelton brought me up well and I've enjoyed my life – until now."

"You heard him," she said. "If he can get her to safety, we have to help him to—"

"Be quiet," Burl said, walking up to them. "You're all talking too much."

Leah snorted and rolled to her feet. She faced up to Burl and slapped his cheek. Burl grunted and moved to grab her hand, but she bunched her fist and slugged him in the stomach. The blow landed without much force, but it caught Burl unawares and he staggered back and to the floor.

Hellfire's men roared with laughter, that sound redoubling as she leaped on Burl and slapped his cheek and then lunged for his hair. She gathered a good grip and began a steady pounding of his head on the floor.

Her action bemused Harvey, but Leah broke off from her fighting to gesture at him, and he realized she had acted foolishly to give him a distraction. So, with everyone's attention on the fight, he took Mollie's hand and led the sleepy girl behind the bar.

Hellfire's men taunted Burl about his poor fighting ability. Then Burl gathered his wits about him. He grabbed Leah's wrists and pushed her up and away from him as he regained his feet.

Harvey took this as his cue and slipped under the bar. The hole through the floor to the underside of the saloon was there and he pushed Mollie into the inky darkness of the hole and jumped down after her.

Below the saloon, the three-foot space provided just enough room to wriggle on his belly. With the smaller Mollie crawling along before him, they headed under the saloon and toward the main drag.

"You've just made a big mistake, woman," Burl said, his voice a few feet above him.

"Burl, you won't hurt her," Hellfire said.

A scuffle sounded, presumably as Burl pushed Leah to the floor. Then more shuffling sounded along with subdued muttering as everyone returned to their former positions.

"Where's the child?" Burl shouted. "And

where's the other one?"

For a moment voices babbled. Then Hellfire called for silence. A long silence dragged on, giving Harvey and Mollie enough time to reach the underside of the boardwalk. Then Hellfire roared with anger.

"Find them!"

Boots appeared before him as a line of men hurried outside, but Harvey continued his steady progress along the underside of the boardwalk. At his side, Mollie whimpered, so he placed a hand over her mouth.

"Can you be real quiet?" he asked.

When she gave a slight nod, Harvey removed his hand and winked at her, and she returned a more confident nod. As Hellfire's men spread out, back in the saloon, raised voices questioned Leah as to where they had gone, but from the tone of Leah's response, Harvey reckoned she was still refusing to acknowledge the question.

Then a cry of triumph sounded, and a hand reached down through the hole behind the bar. Harvey judged that it was only a matter of moments before somebody stuck their head down and saw them.

He confirmed that the men who had left the station weren't visible, so he tugged Mollie's arm and they slipped out from under the boardwalk and stood up. He faced the cage. From inside, Lincoln pointed forward and then over his shoulder, which Harvey took to be the directions Hellfire's men had gone.

Most of them had gone to the store, the most complete of the standing buildings. Nowhere would provide them with a substantial hiding-place, but the nearest building was the station.

Seeing no alternative he scurried past the saloon with his head down and leading Mollie by the hand. The station was so ruined that Hellfire's men hadn't bothered to head down to this end of town.

Harvey edged on to the ruined platform. Then, behind him, the remainder of Hellfire's men clattered out of the saloon. Harvey shuffled into the hulk of the station.

The standing and blackened beams were just a skeleton of the former building.

Even by moonlight they wouldn't provide cover from a search for more than a few seconds. Mollie started to shiver beside him, but whether that was from the night chill or fear Harvey couldn't tell.

He sought out the least dilapidated corner of the station. Two-foot high boards provided protection from casual sight in the moonlight and he kneeled there. He drew Mollie close to him and began a silent prayer that they would be lucky. Then his prayer grew in volume and he directed it toward the only person who could really help them.

"I know you're here," he said. "I need your help and I need it now."

He waited, but no answer came.

"Hellfire will kill me and this girl," he continued. "She's only young and he's already killed her baby sister and she's mighty scared. We need you."

From behind the blackened standing wall,

footsteps approached as Burl clattered on to the station's platform.

"Get over here and bring some light," Burl shouted. "I heard someone talking in the station."

"They're going to find me," Harvey whispered. "I'm betting my life and Mollie's life that you're the only one who can help us. You have to act now or we'll die. Please help us."

All was still in the station. By the lights from farther down the main drag, Burl's shadow fell across the edge of the station building, lengthening as he walked closer. Harvey gritted his teeth, knowing capture was only moments away.

"Please do something," he said.

Two feet to his side, a trapdoor in the floor silently swung open.

FOURTEEN

"You'll never find him," Lincoln shouted through the bars. "Harvey's escaped."

"Be quiet, or your real suffering starts early," Hellfire said, aiming a firm finger at Lincoln.

Lincoln sat down and with a wince he leaned his bruised back against the cage and faced the guards. To have survived one encounter with Hellfire, Harvey must be a resourceful young man – even if he didn't show it when Hellfire had attacked the saloon – and he reckoned that if there were a way to help him, he'd take it.

Trapped in the cage, he saw no opportunity to do anything. He directed taunts at Hellfire's men, hoping to distract them from their search, but they ignored him. After they'd failed to find anyone in the station Hellfire sent men to search down the railroad tracks in both directions, but in the moonlight they found no sign of him or Mollie and soon returned.

With first light just a few hours away, Hellfire called off their search and his men returned to the saloon. He left two men to guard Lincoln's cage, but both men paid little attention to Lincoln.

Raised voices sounded inside the saloon as Hellfire questioning Cooper. From the lawman's scared tone Lincoln judged that it was debatable whether he would live to witness Lincoln's scheduled death at sunup, but after fifteen minutes, the voices petered out.

Shortly after that, snoring sounded from within the saloon. By then the first arc of light was spreading across the eastern horizon. As the light grew an early-morning mist descended, pressing a cold clamminess around him.

The guards grumbled as they paraded back and forth. With increasing frequency they loitered by the fire they'd built to warm themselves. As time passed that grumbling grew and mainly involved the failure of two other men to relieve them.

They debated whether to leave Lincoln to kick that relief awake but then silenced, nudged each other and swung around. Lincoln shuffled around. He hoped that maybe Harvey had gathered the courage to try to help him, but instead a caped figure emerged from the mist-shrouded gloom around the station.

As the figure closed on the cage, it appeared to glide as the cape brushed away the ground mist. A hood hid its face.

"Who in tarnation is this?" one of the guards said.

"It isn't Harvey." The guard narrowed his eyes. "I reckon it's a woman."

"Nobody lives in Calamity."

The other guard placed a hand to his heart. "They don't, but I've heard that the station is haunted."

The other man snorted. "That isn't no ghost."

The figure continued to glide toward them over the mist-shrouded ground.

"Hey, stay back," he shouted.

The figure maintained its steady progress. After another five yards, the man drew his gun, but the figure continued to advance.

"Stay back!"

He raised his gun to shoulder-level and took sight down the barrel. This time the figure halted. Seconds after it had stopped the cape rippled to stillness, but then the figure just stood there, ten yards in front of the guards and to the side of the cage.

"You just saved your life. Now, raise your hands and come here."

The guard stood poised, waiting for it to move, but the figure didn't acknowledge the threat and continued to stand where it was. Lincoln shuffled to the front of the cage, hoping to see who the figure was, but the hood shrouded its face.

"I said, come here," the guard continued.

The figure was like a statue, so the other guard paced forward.

"I've had enough of this," he said.

He stomped to the figure's side and hurled back its hood, but then staggered back a pace, a pained screech escaping his lips. With a swift gesture, the figure replaced the hood before Lincoln could see who it was, but the man still staggered away, his body bent double, his hands framing a knife, which protruded from his chest, the blood gushing over his hands suggesting that whether he removed it or not the blow was fatal.

The other guard stood rigid, his mouth open with silent horror. When the second guard had staggered around in a circle the figure darted forward, whipped the knife from his chest and advanced.

As if this movement broke the first guard from his torpor, he raised his gun, but as he firmed his hand, the figure hurled the knife. The knife flew through the air and hit with deadly accuracy, transfixing his neck.

The gun fell from the man's slack fingers unfired. His hands shot up to his neck, but the torrent of blood cascading over his hands let him do nothing more than utter a pained bleat before he keeled over to sprawl over the other guard.

The figure merely glided toward him and removed the knife. It wiped the blade on the man's jacket, kneeled beside him to remove his key and shuffled toward the cage. With its head lowered, the figure unlocked the cage and stood back.

"I'm obliged," Lincoln said.

He walked his hands up the cage bars until he was standing, suppressing a grunt of pain when his many bruises announced their discomfort. Then he staggered into the doorway and stepped outside.

As the caped figure turned and headed toward the station, only snoring from Hellfire's men came from the saloon, the subdued screams of the guards not having alerted them. Lincoln collected the guns from the dead men and shuffled around to face the saloon.

After his prolonged beating even standing was painful and he had to accept he was in no condition to mount the full-on assault he'd need to free Leah and Cooper. The figure was now closing on the station, but on the edge of the platform it stopped.

The figure turned to Lincoln before continuing. Lincoln shrugged and followed it to the station.

* * *

"Lincoln's escaped," Hellfire said as he stomped to a halt in the saloon doorway. He pointed at Leah. "That means you're going in the cage."

Hellfire stormed across the saloon toward her. Cooper jumped up to block his way, but with a backhanded swipe Hellfire batted him to the floor and grabbed her arm.

"Don't," Leah whined, tearing herself away and then backing until she slammed into the wall. "That had nothing to do with me."

"I reckon it did. You helped Harvey to escape." Hellfire turned on the spot and hurled his hands aloft. "Torch everything. Burn Calamity to the ground."

Hellfire's men ran outside and lit brands. As they scurried from building to building, Hellfire dragged Leah outside. She struggled, but he had a firm grip of her arm as he walked her to the cage.

She threw up a leg and planted it beside the cage door, but Hellfire kicked it away and hurled her into the cage. She swirled around and threw herself at the door, but already Hellfire was slamming it shut.

Burl dragged Cooper outside and then two other men hurled brands into the saloon. Within moments flames were licking at the walls. Then Burl threw Cooper to the ground before the cage.

"Do you still say you don't know what happened here?" Hellfire demanded, kicking Cooper toward the cage.

Cooper rolled to a halt and then shuffled around to face Hellfire.

"I have no idea what's happened to Harvey and Mollie, and I have no idea what's happened to Lincoln."

"Tell me where they are, or I torch this pyre and you can watch your woman go up in flames just like I watched my woman burn."

"I can't answer your question," Cooper said, lowering his head.

Hellfire snorted and walked past him.

"Lincoln, you've got ten minutes," he roared, his voice echoing through the flaming town. "Then this woman dies with Calamity."

Around him, Calamity burned. The long, hot summer had made the buildings tinder-dry. Within minutes every building was alight and flames rippled into the dawn sky to greet the start of a new day.

* * *

Beneath the station building, Lincoln faced the caped figure and settled down. The figure had led him to the station and there, beneath the rubble was where it lived. This had been an underground storeroom, but by the first hints of the lightening sky which were sprinkling around the edges of the trapdoor, it was clear that this person had made a home for itself here.

From the figure's slight stature, Lincoln had decided his savior was a woman. Beyond that, he'd learned nothing. Crates of provisions lined the walls and in one corner stood a rusting cage, its presence hinting at the solution to an old mystery.

In the opposite corner sat the subdued forms of Harvey and Mollie. Lincoln nodded to Harvey and flashed a smile at Mollie, receiving timid smiles in return. Then he turned to the caped figure.

"You seem to have plenty here. Perhaps Shelton Baez didn't need to get any more food for you."

The woman faced him, her hood hiding

her face. Lincoln waited for her to reply, but when she didn't he leaned forward and spoke again.

"Shelton gave Harvey a list of provisions. He was worried about you."

Again Lincoln waited for a response, but again, the darkened hole of the hood just regarded him.

"She won't talk to me," Harvey said. "She did save you and I guess that's all I asked from her."

"I'm obliged, but that still leaves the question of who she is, and I reckon there's only one answer." Lincoln smiled. "You're Adele. The woman Hellfire kidnapped and then fooled himself into believing she cared for him."

Lincoln waited for a reaction and this time, she inclined her head an inch, but whether that was an accident or an agreement, Lincoln couldn't tell.

"You've lived here on your own for sixteen years. Some even think you're a ghost. That's a long time for anyone to keep their own company."

This time Lincoln stayed silent, hoping that his quietness would force an answer from her. By degrees she raised her head, the first light revealing the outline of the face beneath the hood, if not the features.

"Over all that time, you've been Shelton's best customer. So much so that he was prepared to die to keep your identity secret. You've kept him in business by paying handsomely for his help. You used thousands of dollars from the money that was once in that cage."

"It wasn't like that," she said, speaking for the first time, her voice grating, the timbre and the slow way she intoned every word suggesting she seldom spoke.

"I can believe that. Shelton was a good man and would help anyone even if they couldn't pay. So why let everyone think you're dead?"

"Shelton knows why. Others have guessed." She provided an odd snorting sound. "They pretend they don't know."

"Why?"

"Because I want them to," she said, her low tone pleading with Lincoln to desist from his questioning.

"You have nothing to fear from me or from Harvey if that's your reasoning. I know what happened here and I know you weren't with Hellfire willingly. You won't face prison for your part in what happened."

"Prison," she grunted. She pointed at her living-quarters which were as small as the smallest prison cell Lincoln had ever seen.

"Yeah. There's been too much suffering because of what happened here." Lincoln smiled. With his bruised lips, the movement was painful, adding intensity to his plea. "Perhaps it's time for you to end your suffering."

"My suffering will never end."

"I have an idea of what Hellfire might have done to you in the six months before he torched this station."

"Hellfire did nothing but care for me in his own twisted way, but sometimes we make our own hells and our own prisons." She gave her odd snorting sound again. "He didn't burn anything. I torched the station to escape."

Lincoln winced. "It was a good idea even if it failed."

"It wasn't. People burned to death. The unlucky ones survived."

Slowly, she raised a gnarled hand from beneath her cape and grasped the edge of her hood. She removed it and, by the faint light, she revealed the true horror of what being a survivor of this burned station meant.

Mollie screeched and buried her face into Harvey's jacket. Harvey just gulped, but Lincoln met her eyes, the only part of her features that hadn't lost their humanity.

"Just because the fire scarred you, that isn't no reason to hide away."

"It isn't." She ran her hand over the expanse of gnarled scar tissue that now constituted her face and then over a single tress of blond hair, the last vestiges of what would have once been a proud mane. "Down here, I don't have to face what Hellfire made me and he hasn't destroyed me."

"As long as you hide, he has."

She folded the hood back over her face. "Whatever you say, I can't leave."

Lincoln nodded, but then sniffed, reckoning he detected burning. He turned to the trapdoor. In the light emerging around the sides of the door a faint plume of smoke rippled downward.

"I don't reckon you have a choice," he said.

FIFTEEN

Fire raged in Calamity again. This time every building was alight and providing a wall of flames and smoke around the cage. Lincoln kneeled on the side of the trapdoor, judging the extent of the damage and deciding that only the station stood a chance of surviving the inferno.

He ducked down into the hole and cautioned silence, making him wince as his strained back muscles protested. Lincoln shuffled away from the trapdoor. On the platform a man stood with his back to him.

He was torching a heap of wood in the corner of the station. Lincoln walked up to him and with a roll of his shoulders to free the tightness in his muscles he grabbed him from behind. He pulled his arm tight against his throat and held on.

The man struggled, the brand falling from his numb fingers, but Lincoln tightened his grip until the man slumped. Then he let him fall to the ground. As Lincoln stood hunched over taking shallow breaths after his exertions, Harvey climbed out from the hole and stamped around, extinguishing the flames that had already taken hold.

When he'd put out the flames, he and Lincoln had to agree that this building was the only one they could save. Lincoln patted Harvey's back while pointing at the hole and then headed along the platform.

When he didn't hear the trapdoor close behind him he turned. Harvey was removing the gun from the supine man.

"I've got me another gun," he said, hurrying to his side.

Lincoln shook his head. "You'll just get yourself killed, kid. Stay with Adele and Mollie. I'll save the others."

"I'm not a kid, and there are about ten

men out there." Harvey stood tall and rolled his shoulders. "When I last faced them, I did nothing, but not this time. Let me help."

Lincoln weighed up the minor damage this young man could inflict on Hellfire's men against the greater possibility of his getting himself killed, but as he had to admit that in his weak state he was desperate for an advantage, he nodded.

"All right, head around the outskirts of town and come at them from the opposite direction. When I start firing, take out whoever you can and then run."

Harvey beamed with delight and then ran out of town leaving Lincoln to walk on. The smoke swirled and eddied in front of him and he took a deep breath before he waded into it. Lost within the smoke, the town crackled with insistent heat, but with each pace that he took a tapping sounded above the crashing of falling buildings and the shouts of Hellfire's men.

He guessed the tapping came from someone trapped within the cage, and when the smoke cleared before him, Leah was revealed, lying in the cage and beating a worried rhythm on the bars. Marshal Cooper lay sprawled beside the cage, hunched and cradling his bandaged hand as he faced Hellfire and his phalanx of men.

Lincoln walked through the last of the smoke to emerge beside the cage, his gun held down, his gait slow and pained. Ten men stood with Hellfire. With the fire razing Calamity to the ground, there was nowhere where anyone else could hide.

Even so, the odds stacked against him were as impossible as anything he'd faced. Still, he stood before them while searching for a possible advantage that could keep him alive for long enough to kill Hellfire.

One of Hellfire's men turned his way, flinched and then shouted a warning. Before anyone else reacted, Lincoln swung up his gun and ripped gunfire into the men to Hellfire's right side, sending two falling to the ground clutching their chests.

Then he leaped to the side to avoid a

volley of returning gunfire. He groaned as he slapped down on the ground on his side, but he forced himself to keep the roll going toward the saloon.

Slugs blasted around him until he came to a halt on his belly. With his arms outstretched, he fired up, taking another man through the chest. Then the rest scattered, taking positions behind whatever cover they could find.

A burning plank fell from the saloon roof, landing a yard away from Lincoln. With that encouraging the rest of the roof to collapse, he tried to clamber to his feet. The movement proved to be too demanding for him and he succeeded only in getting to his knees. So he crawled along until he was behind the heap of firewood that surrounded the cage.

"Are you all right?" he asked, facing Leah through the bars.

"I'm in a better condition than you are," Leah said. "Is Mollie safe?"

Lincoln turned to the station. "Yeah, she's

safe."

She put a hand to her heart. "Then you have my gratitude, whatever happens next."

Cooper shuffled around the cage to join Lincoln, but his eyes were downcast.

"You did well in that, Lincoln," he said, his voice registering shame. "But I still say you did wrong in endangering us."

"So did you. You should never have helped Hellfire."

"I guess there's no way a man like you would understand what having your family threatened can do to your mind."

"Perhaps I don't, but you have to put it out of your mind and face the likes of Hellfire head on."

"He's right," Leah said from the cage. "Mollie's safe now. We have nothing to lose."

Cooper took a deep breath. Then he firmed his shoulders and turned around. Hellfire and two of his men were hiding behind a heap of wood. Two more men were behind a moldering buggy and two more were behind a barrel. The body of one of the outlaws lay twenty feet away from him.

"Cover me, Lincoln," he said. "It's time I faced the outlaws head on, like you said."

Cooper stayed for long enough to receive a nod from Lincoln. Then he ran off doubled-up. Lincoln straightened up to fire at Hellfire's men and, from the opposite end of town, Harvey chose that moment to help him.

Harvey's gunfire was wild, but the unexpected direction of his shooting caused one man to veer out from behind his cover. Lincoln made him pay for that mistake with a deadly shot to the head as Cooper skidded to a halt beside the body and tore the gun from its hand.

Then he rolled behind the body and, using it as cover, laid down a burst of gunfire at Hellfire's men. With gunfire coming from three different directions, two men were foolish enough to try to get an angle on Cooper and Harvey, but Lincoln and Cooper tore gunfire into them that sprawled them over the buggy.

The remaining men had the sense to realize Harvey was in no danger of inflicting damage on them and they stayed down. When the stable collapsed, spilling burning embers over the hardpan near to the heap of wood Hellfire was hiding behind, Cooper scurried back to rejoin Lincoln beside the cage.

With a few gestures, Cooper and Lincoln agreed that they had severely reduced the number of people they faced and that, for the first time, they stood a chance. Then the remnants of the stable fell in upon itself and a flaming plank fell on to the wood heap, igniting it.

Hellfire had just four men left and three of them were with him behind the heap of wood. As the flames took hold, the heat would force them to come out soon. Then one man did emerge, but when he jumped up he was clutching a burning brand, which he threw toward them.

It flew end over end to bury itself in the

kindling below the cage. Lincoln covered Cooper as he scurried out from the cage and kicked it away, but he wasn't quick enough and the low wind whipped the flames into life.

Within seconds, a fire had shot up around the base of the cage. Inside, Leah screeched and backed into the far corner away from the flames. Lincoln and Cooper grabbed the bars and tried to yank the cage away from the pyre. It was heavy and whenever they managed to put any pressure on it, Hellfire peppered them with gunfire and forced them to relent.

"I have the key," Hellfire shouted. "Hand Lincoln Hawk over, Cooper, and I'll let you have it."

Cooper gritted his teeth. "I'll see you in hell before I hand over a fellow lawman."

Hellfire laughed. "Leah will get there first."

"No she won't," a croaked voice said from behind Lincoln. "You only wanted that money and I have it."

Then Adele emerged from the swirling smoke and headed toward them. Her hood was still over her head, but in her hand was a bulging bag, the weight great enough to make her stumble as she walked through the smoke, heading toward Hellfire.

A smaller shape was shuffling along behind, but Adele was aware that Mollie was following her. She signified that the child should stop, and then continued. As Mollie slumped to sit cross-legged on the ground, Hellfire and his remaining outlaws edged out from their cover.

"Who are you?" Hellfire shouted as Adele glided closer.

"You know who I am, Jeremiah Court," she croaked.

Adele walked past the cage and continued toward Hellfire. The other outlaws covered him, but Hellfire was oblivious to them as he stood before the approaching figure.

"Nobody calls me by that name no more," he said, a smile softening his blemished features. "I'd hoped you were alive, Adele."

"I may not be alive." She stopped twenty feet before the burning heap of wood and dropped the bag at her feet. "But I survived."

"Have you returned to me?"

"No. I'm just here to give you what you really wanted."

She kicked the bag over, the open top spilling a flurry of bills to the ground. The breeze fluttered several bills away for them to fly into the flames and burn. Hellfire's men boggled at the money, but Hellfire ignored it.

"You're wrong. I never wanted anything but you."

Adele gave her odd snorting sound through the ruined mass of tissue that was her nose and then reached up to remove the hood from her head. The men around Hellfire snarled, their lips curling with distaste, but Hellfire just smiled.

"You're just as beautiful as I remember," he said, walking toward her.

"You're just as deluded as I remember."

"That's only when I'm with you."

He stopped before Adele, still smiling, and then reached out to finger the ridged edges of her scarred cheeks. Adele flinched back and then reached down to the bag.

"You don't want this money?" She held it to the side, closer to the flames, more bills spilling out to catch stray sparks and burn.

Behind Hellfire, his men shrugged and gulped.

"I don't want that. I just want you."

She nodded and slipped her other hand into her cloak. When it emerged, she clutched her knife.

"Watch out!" Burl cried, breaking into a run.

Hellfire raised a hand, his eyes never leaving hers.

"My woman would never harm me."

Adele lunged, the point of the knife brushing Hellfire's chest, but Burl tore gunfire into her, the slugs ripping into her chest and knocking her back for her to crash to the ground. The bag flew from her hand to land on the edge of the flames.

"Adele!" Hellfire cried as she writhed.

Then he turned around and hammered lead at Burl and the other men. Burl fell backward, his chest holed. The others ran for the bag. Hellfire killed two before they'd managed a single pace.

As the last man threw himself to the ground Hellfire fired at him. The man slid to a halt with his fingers just inches from the bag before he bit the dirt. Then Hellfire hurled his gun away and fell to his knees to cradle Adele in his arms.

Beside the cage Lincoln considered the scene. In his grief Hellfire had eliminated everyone; the only danger now came from his own grief-torn form and the burning pyre.

"Hellfire, the key," Lincoln shouted.

Hellfire stood up with the dying Adele cradled and sprawled backward over his arm.

"Give it to him," Adele said, her voice pained and fading. "Then we can be together."

Hellfire gave a frantic nod and then placed her on the ground to rummage through his pockets. He found the key and held it out, but it fell from his trembling fingers. While Lincoln covered him, Cooper broke into a run.

He threw himself to the ground, sliding over the dirt as he scooped up the key. Then he hurled it over his shoulder to Lincoln, who moved as quickly as he could manage to the cage.

Lincoln side-stepped through the flames to the door, thrust the key in the lock and hurled open the door. Leah leaped through the advancing flames, tumbling over Lincoln in her haste to escape.

As they rolled clear of the cage Cooper joined them. He hugged her, but when they stood back, Hellfire had abandoned Adele and was picking a route past the burning debris of the collapsed roof to enter the saloon.

Lincoln would have let him go to meet his death in whichever way he chose, but thrust under one arm was the small shape of Mollie. Cooper moved to follow him, but Lincoln took his arm and signified that he should stay and keep Leah safe.

Then he shuffled on, forcing his aching muscles to move quickly. When he reached the saloon he tore his jacket from his back so that he had something to put over his face and protect himself from the flames.

Even so, he had to step through a growing wall of flame to enter the saloon. As he hurled the flaming jacket away from him and batted embers from the rest of his clothes, he faced Hellfire, who stood in the center of the saloon, the flames rippling around him, the child in his arms.

"Are you ready to kill an unarmed man, Lincoln?" he asked.

"I will if I have to, but put down the child," Lincoln said. "This is about you and me, like I told you it always would be."

"I know that, but you have a weakness, Lincoln. You care about people."

"I do, but so do you. I saw what you did

for Adele." Lincoln raised his gun and, standing sideways, aimed at Hellfire's head.

"Now it all means nothing." Hellfire rocked up on his heels and then down, the action shaking the weakening floor. "You may be prepared to kill me, Lincoln, but when I die, I'll fall through the floor and drop this child into the flames. That'll be enough to stop you firing."

Lincoln frowned, but then Harvey spoke up from behind him, having braved the flames, too.

"It'll stop him, but not me," he said.

"Get out of here, Harvey," Lincoln snapped.

Harvey ignored his demand as he edged around the collapsed and burning bar to stand in front of Hellfire. He held his hands wide apart.

"I should have died sixteen years ago," Harvey said. "So kill me, not her."

"You survived the station fire, too?" Hellfire said.

"No. I wasn't even born then, but my

mother did and she lived long enough to give birth to me."

"Nobody survived that fire other than Shelton and Adele." Hellfire shook himself. "Are you saying that. . . ?"

"I'm not saying nothing other than I don't fear you no more and I don't need no ghosts to help me." He took a long pace toward Hellfire. "Put her down for no other reason than I asked you to."

Hellfire's blemished face softened. He removed a locket from his neck and looped it over Mollie's head. Then he patted her on the top of her head and placed her on the floor at his feet.

The moment his hands left her, Lincoln fired a shot that slammed between Hellfire's eyes. Hellfire toppled over backward, landing on his back and crashing through the burning boards.

Lincoln had fired at the earliest possible moment and Mollie teetered on the edge of the hole, her arms wheeling as she fought for balance. As a burst of flame erupted from the hole, Harvey was at her side, scooping her into his arms. He stood over the fiery hole into which Hellfire had plummeted and then hurried back toward Lincoln.

"Come on," Lincoln said, pointing at the burning saloon. "Just because he's staying in hell, it doesn't mean we have to."

SIXTEEN

Lincoln and Harvey picked their way outside to find that Leah and Marshal Cooper were standing before the saloon. Leah took Mollie in her arms and while the family enjoyed being reunited, Lincoln headed off to secure the bag of money.

It was no longer there. Unlike last time, this time its fate was clear – a smoldering heap of paper. The stable fire had grown to consume the bag and although Lincoln judged that if he braved the flames again, he might be able to save some of the money, he turned away.

Harvey had hunkered down beside Adele. Lincoln joined him and examined her, noting that thick blood coated her cape and it was still spreading.

"How bad is it?" she said through scarred lips.

"It's not looking good," Lincoln said, dropping down to his knees beside Harvey.

"Then take me back to the station. It didn't burn and it's sunup soon."

Lincoln nodded and moved to help her stand, but Harvey brushed Lincoln away.

"No," he said. "You've spent sixteen years hiding under that station. You should see the sun come up with me this time."

Harvey drew her around to face eastward. With Harvey cradling her against his chest, she murmured another request to Lincoln to take her back to the station, but he ignored her plea and stood back.

Together, Harvey and Adele watched the sun rise, but at what point she stopped watching, Lincoln didn't notice. As Calamity's flames began to die, he rejoined Harvey.

"You were good to her at the end," he said.

"I was hoping she might be my mother

and maybe. . . ."

The things that Harvey had said to Hellfire had confused Lincoln at the time and the reason Hellfire had obeyed Harvey's request to put Mollie down had confused him even more. Back then, he had just been pleased that Harvey had found a distraction that enabled them to save Mollie, but now he realized what Harvey had meant.

It was an idea that could tear a man apart if he considered it too deeply. As knowing the truth might be worse than never knowing it, Lincoln shook his head.

"It's unlikely, but at least it was a big enough possibility to surprise Hellfire."

"Perhaps it was. I've seen her often in my life, standing on the ridge and watching over the trading post, almost as if she was looking out for me." Harvey patted Adele's shoulder. "Do you know who she was?"

Lincoln sighed. "I don't, but she was somebody's wife or somebody's mother or somebody's daughter, or maybe she was just everyone that died here."

Harvey nodded and laid Adele's body on her back.

"Then come on. I've got to find Shelton."

Lincoln nodded, figuring that was a matter he should explain only when they were out of town. He moved past the reunited Cooper family and then through the smoldering and burned-out remains of Calamity.

The town had finally died today and there was nothing left here for any of them. So Lincoln flexed his arms and then picked up the body of the woman whom Hellfire had kidnapped and kept prisoner for six months, a woman who had been pregnant during the station fire, a woman who had survived and lived on for another sixteen years.

As gently as he could, he laid her over a spare horse. Then with the others he headed out of Calamity and, just as he'd done sixteen years ago, rode down the side of the railroad tracks in search of what a new day would bring him.

RAIDERS OF THE MISSION SAN JUAN

Scott Connor

Marshal Lincoln Hawk is on the trail of the Shannon gang when he learns to his surprise that they have already been killed. He alone believes that the dead outlaws have been incorrectly identified, so he continues on the owlhoot trail. . . .

His search leads him to the Mission San Juan where he finds the gang still very much alive as they prepare to claim a stash of Mexican gold.

They will stop at nothing to protect their alibi and no help is forthcoming from the peaceful mission padres.

Can Lincoln hold his own when faced with an army of gun-toting raiders?

5th in the Lincoln Hawk Series

CULBIN PRESS

Printed in Great Britain
by Amazon

79325402R00130